LoCK-iN

the misadventures of Willie Plummet

PAUL BUCHANAN
& ROD RANDALL

CPH
SAINT LOUIS

The Misadventures of Willie Plummet

Cover illustration by John Ward.
Back cover photo by Ira Lippke.
Cover and interior design by Karol Bergdolt.

Scripture quotations are taken from the HOLY BIBLE, NEW INTERNATIONAL VERSION®. NIV®. Copyright ©1973, 1978, 1984 by International Bible Society. Used by permission of Zondervan Publishing House. All rights reserved.

Copyright © 2001 Rod Randall
Published by Concordia Publishing House
3558 S. Jefferson Avenue, St. Louis, MO 63118-3968

Manufactured in the United States of America

Library of Congress Cataloging-in-Publication Data

Buchanan, Paul, 1959–
    Lock-In / by Paul Buchanan and Rod Randall.
       p. cm.— (The misadventures of Willie Plummet)
      Summary: In honor of the eighth-graders' graduation, Willie's church
is holding a Lock-In, including an exciting contest that might also
introduce some of the participants to Jesus.
    ISBN 0-570-07130-5
    [1. Contests—Fiction. 2. Christian life—Fiction.] I. Randall, Rod, 1962-
II. Title.
    PZ7.B87717 Lo 2001
    [Fic]—dc21

1 2 3 4 5 6 7 8 9 10   10 09 08 07 06 05 04 03 02 01

For all of Willie's fans,
thanks for making
so many adventures possible

Contents

The Mighty IQs

I sprinted with the rest of the IQs down Main Street. Too many streetlights, way too many. We needed to hide—and fast. Our feet beat the pavement. At Sally's Salon we ducked into the dark passageway beside the building.

"Are they coming?" I asked, breathing hard.

Chet poked his head around the corner. His black beanie matched his long sleeved T-shirt. "All clear, IQs. We're good!" He put his arms in the air like he'd just won a gold medal. "Is this our night or what?"

We didn't say anything; Chet got on us. "What happened to *You bet, Chet*? Let's hear it!" He wanted us to answer with *You bet, Chet* whenever he asked us a question. That would prove we had spirit.

Chet jumped around and headed for the wall. He ran two steps up it then did a back flip.

I cupped my hand over Felix's ear. "This guy's in a league of spazz all his own."

"Cool, huh?" Felix replied. "Between his spirit and our inventions, we've got it made in the shade."

Chet was our chaperon for the Lock-In. He was also a spirit leader at the state university. No surprise there.

Felix took off his backpack and kneeled beside it. He was my best friend and liked inventing stuff as much as I did. I hovered over him as he unzipped the main pouch. He picked over the flashlight, remote control truck, and other gadgets we had brought along.

I reached in and grabbed a small container. "What's this?"

"Sneezing powder," Felix told me. "Don't—"

Too late. I peeked under the lid.

"*Ah-Choo!*" My face erupted in a giant sneeze. Then another. "*Ah-Choo!*"

"Bless you," Megan said.

I started to thank her, but sneezed again. In her face.

Megan wiped her cheeks and eyes.

"Sorry," I said, feeling like a total clod.

Megan has light brown hair and a pretty smile. For some reason, whenever she's around life just seems better. Normally, I'm trying to impress her ... not sneeze on her.

Felix grabbed the container and pressed the lid tight. "I finished the formula last night. Cool, huh?"

I couldn't believe it. Felix had snuck in an invention even I didn't know about.

Chet squeezed my shoulders like I was a prize fighter. "Feeling better, Champ? You're up."

"Maybe someone else should try this one," I suggested. "What if I sneeze on them?"

"Come on, Willie," Felix urged. "They know you. Your hobby store is just four doors down."

I shook my red head. "No way. It's a *beauty parlor*. I've been in there, like once, to look for my sister. If they're not part of the Lock-In, I'll look like a total chump."

"So what's new?" Felix shrugged.

"Just go," Leonard "Crusher" Grubb said. He jabbed me with his thick fingers. "Don't be a wuss."

I let out a sigh. Why couldn't Crusher be on another team? When they told us to form groups of six, Felix and I got together right away. Then we grabbed Sam. She's one of our closest friends and tends to end up on most of our misadventures. Next we asked Megan and her brother Mitch to join us. We were looking for one more person when Joe, our youth pastor, stepped up with Leonard, the bully of Glenfield Middle School. Joe didn't tell us why Crusher would be on our team, but it was obvious. No one else wanted him.

Mitch pulled down his beanie to cover his blond hair. Then he unfolded the riddle sheet from under his arm. "Remember, it's 'Iggy, Iggy, Iggy, have you seen my piggy?' She'll respond with, 'Orky, Orky, Orky, yes, I've seen your porky.' Then, we get our prize."

"If we're in the right place," I added. I looked at Sam for moral support but didn't get any. She stared at nothing, and her lips mumbled silent words.

I nudged her arm. "Stop worrying about your testimony. You'll do fine."

Sam told me she couldn't help it, but would try.

Suddenly Megan covered her mouth with one hand and pointed toward the alley with the other. "I saw someone back there."

Chet told us to get down. He crept to the end of the building. His head turned up and down the alley. "All clear."

"Come on, Willie, go for it!" Megan urged with a smile.

That's all it took. Megan had spoken. I popped a mint in my mouth, rushed across the sidewalk, and pushed through the door. Felix and Mitch followed. The rest of our team stayed outside.

A woman with gobbed on pink lipstick came over from her station. Her name tag read "Gladys." She smacked her gum with an attitude, like the gum had it coming to it. Felix pressed behind me.

"Can I help you?" Gladys asked.

My tongue ballooned in my mouth. I chewed up the mint and swallowed it. "Um ... Iggy, Iggy ... something, piggy."

Gladys smirked. "Excuse me?"

Felix scolded me in a whisper. "Three Iggies, then *have you seen* my piggy."

I cleared my throat and tried again. I made it through the Iggies. But instead of, *have you seen,* I asked *will you be.*

For some reason those three words made a big difference. Big big.

There was nothing glad about Gladys. The gum dropped from her mouth. "What did you call me?"

Red heat flowed to my forehead. "Um ... nothing."

Felix and Mitch backed away from me.

Gladys glanced in a mirror then at me. "Are you saying I'm fat?"

I shook my head so fast my teeth rattled. I started to explain that we were participating in a church Lock-In, but Gladys didn't let me finish. She gave me an earful.

Sally came over and put her hands on her hips. "Don't I know you?"

I stalled. "Um ..."

Felix stepped forward. "Sure you know him. He's Willie Plummet. His parents own the hobby store down the street."

"Really?" Gladys said. She exchanged a frown with Sally. "I'm calling your parents first thing in the morning. Now get out." She came toward me.

I backed away, bumping into Felix. He pressed into Mitch and we all squeezed through the door at the same time and tumbled onto the sidewalk. The other IQs rushed over. Felix couldn't wait to tell everyone what happened.

"Will you be my piggy?" Megan mocked. She giggled and covered her mouth.

Sam looked at Megan and they laughed together. "Smooth, Willie. Real smooth."

"I told you I didn't know it," I complained. "I've had too many finals. I can't think straight."

"You've got to," Felix said. "This is our big night, the one we've dreamed about since grade school. This night was made for us!"

Felix was right. In just a couple of days, our junior high years would come to an end. We would complete our finals, clean out our lockers, and say good-bye to Glenfield Middle School. To help us celebrate, our church put on a giant Lock-In for all the graduating eighth-graders. It was a huge outreach event. Kids who would never normally come to church showed up. Kids like Crusher. Some even heard about Jesus for the first time.

The Lock-In began with registration and dinner. Then we divided into teams and met our chaperons. It was Chet's idea that we call ourselves IQs. He came up with a cheer about how the mighty IQs never lose.

Each team was given a piece of paper with eight clues that led to eight different locations. At each location we had to repeat the Iggy, Iggy rhyme. If the person answered with the Orky, Orky part, we were in the right place and would get a prize. The first team to return to the church with all eight prizes would be the winner.

But that was easier said than done.

"What was the first riddle again?" I asked Mitch.

He unfolded the piece of brown paper, burnt on the edges to resemble a treasure map. "Beauty is only skin deep."

I shrugged, frustrated. "It has to be a beauty parlor. Unless—"

"Secret Police!" Chet blurted out.

We all dropped to our knees and crawled back to the passageway. The SPs were high schoolers from our church youth group. Their job was to capture kids and take them to the Pen, a fenced-in playground at our church.

We huddled next to the building. Chet started to look, but Felix pulled him back.

"They might see you. Here." He reached into his backpack and pulled out a small radio antenna with a mirror taped to the end. The tiny mirror reflected the street. "They're still there."

While Felix kept an eye out, I brought up my idea from earlier. "What about the pharmacy? It would have skin treatment stuff?"

"Makes sense," Megan admitted. "They'd have make-up."

"And lotions," Sam said.

"And stuff for zits," Mitch added.

We all looked at him.

"At least that's what I've heard," he quickly put in. "Tell 'em Megan."

She slugged her brother. "You tell them. How would I know?"

"They're getting close," Felix warned us.

Chet went spastic. He brought a finger to his lips to shush us. He waved the other hand to make sure we understood.

We crouched lower and held our breaths—everyone except Crusher. He just rolled his eyes and looked at the alley, like he wanted to ditch us.

"They turned around," Felix said. He studied the mirror a while longer. "They're gone."

"Well, Plummet?" Crusher elbowed me. "Are you going or not?"

After the fiasco in the beauty parlor, I wanted to say, "Or not."

Chet squeezed beside Felix and asked if it was clear.

Felix turned the mirror in all directions. "You bet, Chet. Come on, Willie. Ready. Set. Go!"

I bolted from the alley. Crossed the sidewalk. I jumped the curb and darted between two parked cars. Midway into the street the siren wailed. An angry shout turned my head. The red light of a police car stopped me cold.

Jaywalker Blues

Locked up for the lock-in. I couldn't believe it, but here I was in the Glenfield town jail. Felix had done it again.

The police officer had caught up with me on the other side of the street and read me the riot act. At first I thought it was a joke. But not for long. I had jaywalked and the officer wasn't about to let me off the hook. Chet came over and explained that we were participating in a church game, but that didn't help. Even the whole team pleading on my behalf wasn't enough. The officer sat me in the back of the squad car and pulled away.

I clutched the bars and stared at the door that led down a corridor. The front desk and lobby were beyond that. I expected the door to fling open and my teammates to rush to my defense at any second.

Make that minute.

Hour?

I sat down feeling glum. The thin mattress barely covered the bottom bunk. The rest of the furniture included a plastic chair, toilet, and sink. Someone had scratched marks on the wall that I guessed stood for days. I counted 23.

I lay back on the bed and closed my eyes. I prayed for the Lord's help, not just to get me out, but to help our team win. I opened my eyes and stared at the cement wall. I scanned over initials, rude words, then finally settled on two lines. A cross. It was crooked and faint, painted over, but it was still there. I traced it with my finger and thought about the cross Jesus died on. That put things in perspective.

For weeks Pastor Joe had told us that the Lock-In was mainly about reaching kids with the Gospel. That's what mattered. Crusher had never come to a youth event before, but here he was. Instead of being glad, I was frustrated that he was on our team. I closed my eyes and prayed for forgiveness. From there, I prayed for Crusher, that his heart would be open to the message of Christ presented later in the night. I also lifted up Sam and her testimony. I asked that she wouldn't be nervous and that the Lord would speak through her as she shared her own story of faith. I also prayed that Sam's dad would get back from his business trip in time to hear her.

My eyes were still closed when I heard keys in a lock at the end of the corridor. I moved to the front of the cell. A police officer came toward me, one that knew me ... well.

Officer Sutton was tall and all muscle. He made a tisk tisk sound and shook his head. "Mr. Willie Plummet. What a surprise."

I quickly told him about our Lock-In and that I was trying to solve a clue. "Do you think you could pull a few strings and get me out?"

"You? A convicted criminal?" Officer Sutton glanced over the papers he was holding. "I liked it better when you were catching the crooks."

"Me too," I agreed. "Was that guy convicted?" Earlier in the year someone tried to burglarize Classic Coins, the shop next door to my parents' hobby store. Felix, Sam, and I caught the guy in the act and helped Officer Sutton put him behind bars.

Officer Sutton watched me, his expression firm. "On all counts. You probably think that means I owe you one."

I nodded.

Officer Sutton didn't. "Jaywalking may seem like a small thing, but if you were hit by a car, it wouldn't be."

He asked me if I understood, and I told him that I did. He went on about how laws are for our protection and breaking them puts ourselves and others in danger. When he finished, he had another look at the report in his hands then headed for the door. "I'll see what I can do."

He was only gone for a few seconds when the door flew open again. Felix lead the IQs down the corridor.

"Dude, you really did it this time," Felix said.

"Me!" I grabbed his shirt through the bars. "You're the one who told me to run. You and your mirror."

Felix twisted away and straightened his shirt. "No wonder they locked you up. You're dangerous." He told everyone to get back and laughed while he said it. He talked about getting me moved to a padded cell.

I reached as far as I could through the bars, but couldn't get a hold of him.

Felix loved that. He laughed and moved within an inch of my fingertips. "Ooo ... I'm so scared." He danced around and made faces at me.

"Would you guys knock it off," Sam said. I thought she was going to give me an earful about running into the street in front of the police car. But she didn't. "Why couldn't this happen to me?"

I nearly choked. "To you? Why would you—"

"Because then I'd have something to talk about in my testimony," Sam blurted out. "My life's boring."

"No way," I said. "I can't wait to hear you." I squeezed the solid steel bars. "If I can."

"Don't worry about a thing," Chet told me. "No cell can hold an IQ down." He kicked into spirit leader mode. "Remember the movie?" He clapped and started to chant. "Free Willy! Free Willy!"

Everyone rolled their eyes.

Mitch leaned in and shared some good news with me. "You were right about the pharmacy. We got our first prize."

"Let's see it," I said.

Crusher stepped up. "Only if you wear it."

"Huh?"

Chet explained. "When they gave us the prize, we found out that one person in our group has to be the Clue Catcher."

"The what?" I asked.

"The Clue Catcher," Felix said. "A team member who will wear everything we receive. The IQs took a quick vote, and we picked you."

"That's 'cause I wasn't there," I whined.

"Pretty smart, huh?" Felix smiled. He pointed at his brain. "That's why they call us IQs." Mitch produced a pair of fake glasses with a big rubber nose attached. A bushy black mustache hung from the nose.

"No way," I griped. "Call my lawyer. I'm staying here all summer." I started for the bunk, but Megan reached in and grabbed my shoulder.

"Come on, Willie," she urged. "Just wear them. I bet they'll look cute on you."

I shook it off, but for some reason I never made it to the bunk. Before long I was trying them on. "Well?"

Everyone cracked up.

Crusher even let out a laugh. "You're the man, Plummet."

I raised an eyebrow and held my chin, pretending to be an intellectual. "It's nothing, really." I stared at the ceiling, like I was pondering a deep thought. I was so into my antics, I didn't notice who had returned.

"Are you finished?" Officer Sutton asked.

I quickly removed the glasses and plastic nose. "Um ... yeah."

Officer Sutton stepped to the cell. "I convinced the arresting officer that I owe you one." He unlocked the cell and the heavy steel door slid open. "No more jaywalking. Right?"

"Right," I said.

He had my team promise to keep an eye on me. "Now what's this about a mystery hunt?"

We filled him in.

Felix went on and on about my mix-up in the beauty parlor.

"You asked her be your piggy?" Officer Sutton cringed. He wanted to see our clues.

Mitch handed them over.

"These could lead you anywhere," Officer Sutton said. "I guess I shouldn't be surprised if kids show up here." He gave the list back to Mitch and told us we were free to leave.

We made our way through the lobby and out the front door before I stopped. "Wait a second. Let me see that list!"

I scanned the clues and stopped on the third. "*Admission by ticket only*. We're here!"

Felix didn't think so. "No way. Movie theater."

"Think about it," I insisted. "A ticket just put me in jail. Who goes to jail for a jaywalking ticket?" I hurried back in the lobby followed by the IQs.

"Now what?" Officer Sutton asked. He looked annoyed.

I cleared my throat. "Iggy, Iggy, Iggy, have you seen my piggy?"

His face turned to stone. He glanced at the officer at the desk then back at me. "Mr. Plummet, for the last time ... Orky, Orky, Orky, yes, I've seen your porky."

"Oh, yeah!" Chet hollered. He nearly hit the ceiling.

Felix joined him. So did Mitch and Megan.

Officer Sutton went behind the counter and returned with a purple top hat. "For you."

I tried it on along with the plastic nose and glasses. "Now who's the coolest kid on the team?"

"You are, Sir Willie," Megan said. "Quite so."

I was still soaking up the attention when Officer Sutton got on the radio. "SPs, huh? You're sure?" He lowered the handset and addressed our group. "If I were you, I'd get out of here. Now!"

Down But Not Out

I hurried down the street after the group, trying to keep up. I kept one hand on the fake nose and the other on the top hat. According to the rules, I had to wear all of the objects at all times. Felix didn't slow down for me, either. After leaving the police station, he took one look at the clue sheet and decided that he had solved number two.

"Wait up!" I called after him.

He didn't. But Crusher did. He even dropped behind me. I asked him if he was all right. He ignored me at first, then muttered something about how dumb this was. I encouraged him to stick with us, that it would get better. Suddenly, my glasses and top hat didn't mean much. I just kept looking back at Leonard and praying that he wouldn't leave.

Felix finally stopped in front of Sir Quick Print Shop. The IQs huddled around him. I breathed a sigh of relief. I had worked for the owner, Mr. Adams, ear-

lier in the year. I used a team of dogs and my special-
ly invented Sidewalk Dogsled to deliver his print jobs.
The Sidewalk Dogsled was the talk of the town and
even made the front page of the newspaper.

I tried the front door. Locked. I moved over and
peered through the window. Mr. Adams stood behind
the counter talking to a customer. The man turned. It
was Steve Crubble, the guy who ran the Bait Shack at
Lunker Lake. He flipped through a brochure and
shook his head. He seemed frustrated.

"I think we're in the wrong place," I said.

"Just knock," Crusher said.

"Why would Mr. Adams lock the front door if he
was part of the Lock-In?" I asked.

"You can do it, Champ," Chet said. He rubbed my
neck.

I stood behind Felix and read the second clue.
Dries quick. Looks slick. Goes on thick.

Felix reasoned that the locked front door was
probably just a diversion. "*Dries quick* must mean
ink. And ink looks slick."

"What about *Goes on thick?*" I countered. "Ink
isn't thick."

Mitch backed Felix. "Actually, some ink is really
thick, like the stuff they put on T-shirts."

"Who here thinks this is the right place?" Felix
counted the raised hands. Mine was the only one that
didn't go up.

I straightened my fake glasses and purple top hat, then knocked on the window.

Mr. Adams squinted in our direction and made his way over. Instead of unlocking the front door, he pulled the blinds.

"That's weird," Felix muttered. He tried the door himself. The knob didn't turn, but the door pushed in. "What'd I tell you? Now go get 'em, Tiger."

Crusher and Mitch gave me a shove. I stumbled inside the door.

"Get back!" Mr. Crubble shouted.

I saw green. Rows of teeth. Mr. Crubble's alligator, Molly!

I scrambled back toward the door. But this time it closed. Tight.

I couldn't get out.

The giant alligator came at me. Jaws opened. Teeth dripping.

"Easy, Molly," Mr. Crubble commanded. "Easy, girl." He stepped over and picked up the alligator's leash. After a few gentle tugs, Molly moved back.

Mr. Adams rushed around and opened the door. He chewed me out in front of everyone. "Since when do you barge through a locked door?"

I shot a harsh glance at Felix, then explained what we were doing. Mr. Adams calmed down, but not much. He told us that Mr. Crubble had stopped by with Molly to pose for a brochure. I could tell Mr. Adams was pretty uncomfortable having an alligator in his shop. I didn't blame him. I still shivered when I remembered seeing Molly in Lunker Lake.

Mr. Adams exhaled real slow and let his eyes drift from person to person. He finished with me and managed a smile. "Willie, it's late, and I should have been home an hour ago." He stepped back inside and this time the door latched.

"Way to go, Sherlock," I said to Felix.

He defended his conclusion, and asked me if I had any better ideas.

"Yeah," I told him. "You wear this stuff. That way I can solve the clues and you can look like a dope."

I felt bad for jumping all over Felix, but after getting locked up, laughed at, and left behind, I was starting to get annoyed.

"Can't switch," Chet said. "One person has to wear everything. We already picked you."

"Why can't we appoint a new person?" I asked. "Maybe they just don't want you to split the stuff up between the team."

Chet reread the rule sheet then flipped it over. His finger scanned the words as he mumbled. "Maybe it's okay. It doesn't say a new person can't be appointed."

I started with the top hat. Then I gladly handed Felix the fake glasses, nose, and mustache.

"But I already wear glasses," Felix complained. He put them on anyway.

For some reason no one laughed at Felix like they did me.

"Maybe I should wear everything," Sam suggested. She tucked her blonde hair behind her ear. "Then at least I'd have something to talk about in my testimony."

"No way. We're good," Chet said. He had us look at the clue list while he kept an eye out for SPs.

"Wait a second," Megan said. "*Dries quick. Looks slick. Goes on thick.* What if it's paint instead of ink?"

"The paint store," Felix said. "Let's try it!"

Everyone agreed and we took off. At first Felix led the way. Then he dropped back to adjust the fake glasses. A painful cry followed. The IQs wheeled around. Felix held his ankle and rolled from side to side.

Everyone rushed over.

Except me. Guilt held me back. My feet felt like they were in cement blocks. Felix had never done well in sports. The backpack was heavy enough. Why did I have him wear the prizes?

Chet kneeled beside Felix. I came over just as Felix put weight on his foot. He winced and quickly lifted it off the ground.

Sam squatted to examine Felix's ankle. "Did you hear it break?"

Felix shook his head. "It's just sprained. No big deal."

Crusher gave me a shove. "Way to go, Plummet."

"I knew you shouldn't have switched," Mitch added.

I apologized and took the prizes back. Everyone focused on Felix. They knew how much this night meant to him. Now he would hardly be able to walk, forget about running from place to place. We debated over what to do. Sam thought we should go back to church and explain the situation to Joe. Felix offered to turn himself in so we could continue. No one would hear of it.

"How bad is it?" Chet asked.

Felix put weight on his ankle again. This time he hobbled around. "It's not bad. I can walk it off." His face didn't agree. His eyes narrowed and his cheeks tightened.

"You oughta wrap it," Crusher said.

"Crutches would be good," Mitch put in. "And ice."

I thought for a moment then got an idea. "We might have those things at Plummet's Hobbies."

Chet and Mitch got on opposite sides of Felix and we headed for the store.

~~~

My dad sat behind the register reading a hobby magazine. One look at me and he smirked. "I like the nose-job, Son. But the mustache has got to go." When he realized Felix was hurt, he came over.

My mom appeared from the back room followed by Phoebe, my 10-year-old next-door neighbor.

"What are you doing here?" I asked Phoebe.

She giggled at the sight of me. "Who cares about me? Look at you."

My mom covered her mouth to hide her smile. My parents and Phoebe had heard enough about the Lock-In to know what was going on. I filled them in about the police station and Felix's ankle.

"I'm sure there's an Ace bandage back there," my mom said. She joined my dad beside Felix. They both seemed certain it was just a sprain.

"I think there are some crutches there too," my dad called after me.

Phoebe tagged along as I headed for the back room.

"Orville and Amanda are out doing stuff, so I'm helping your parents." Phoebe avoided my eyes. "They thought it might get busy."

"On a Friday night?" I questioned. Phoebe was acting kind of strange, but I had more important things to think about. I shifted my attention to the back room, the place Felix and I call the lab. It's where our inventions come together. The discarded parts and open boxes from the hobby store come in real handy. I found an ice pack in the freezer and asked Phoebe to take it to Felix. I started looking for the Ace bandage on some shelves. I pushed aside model kits, balsa wood, books, and paints, but came up empty. Eventually, the rest of the IQs joined me.

So did Phoebe.

Felix sat on the lab table with the ice bag on his ankle.

"What's this?" Megan asked. She kneeled beside a steel shelf.

Felix answered her. "That's the Video Sub. We used it to catch the poacher of Lunker Lake."

Phoebe wanted everyone to know that it was *her* video camera that fit inside the submarine.

"Check this out," Crusher said. He picked up a human-size locust mask that Sam and I had made. It had giant black eyes and a lopsided antenna.

"Put that one away," Felix moaned. "Wiseguy Willie had me wear it to attract bugs."

"Not just any bugs," I added. "Ballistic bugs."

I laughed and told them everything I had gone through to try and win the Bug-Off at the Locust Festival. "The prize for first place was $5,000."

Mitch put on the mask and made a loud buzzing sound. He reached for Sam.

She laughed and ran away. "Have fun getting that off."

She was right. Mitch's arms flexed and strained as he wrestled with the mask. He finally freed himself with a *pop*.

"I should have learned my lesson after the Founder's Day Parade," Mitch admitted. As part of his

costume for our school float, he had worn an old
scuba diving hood painted like a blueberry. It didn't
want to come off either.

We kept looking, but couldn't find the Ace bandage or crutches anywhere. Crusher even checked
the bathroom. He came out with a roll of toilet paper.
"Here, Paterson. Wrap your ankle with this."

I grabbed the roll and started for Felix's ankle.
"Come on, Dude. It's squeezably soft—and double-
ply."

"Knock it off," he said, pushing me away. "It's not
strong enough."

Sam got in the act. "Use two rolls."

"Or three," Megan added.

"We can TP your whole leg!" Chet cheered. He
jumped up and kicked his foot above his head.

"Or body," Crusher put in.

We might have kept going, but Phoebe caught our
attention. "Over here." She had been digging around
in the back corner behind a stack of boxes. When we
got to her, she was squatting beside my greatest
invention ever, the Skyrunner 1000. It was a remote
control flying machine that resembled part helicopter
and part lawn mower. With helium balloons attached,
it flew like a flying saucer. Just ask our town. When
people first saw it, they thought some sort of invasion
from planet X had come to Glenfield.

"I wondered where that thing ended up," Sam
said.

I patted the Skyrunner 1000.

Megan pointed behind me. "What's that?"

I pushed a lab coat aside and sure enough, a pair of crutches leaned in the corner.

Felix grabbed the crutches and hurried to the center of the lab. "Forget about the Ace bandage. I'm okay. Let's go." He reminded us that with only two clues solved, we had less than an hour to solve six more.

That got our attention. Megan held the wrinkled clue sheet and we gathered around. A chorus of mumbling filled the lab as we strained our brains.

My mom came in the back room to check on us. In no time she found the Ace bandage. She wrapped it around Felix's ankle and told him to stay off it. Then she pulled me aside. "Keep everyone quiet. And when you leave, go out the back way."

"How come?" I asked.

She didn't answer. She cracked open the door to the front just enough to allow her body to pass through.

Phoebe took that as her cue to follow. But she shoved the door all the way open. I noticed Orville with a friend talking to my dad. At first I didn't think much of it. Then I read the front of Orville's shirt. The words left me speechless. Secret Police.

Our eyes met just before the door closed and I heard him shout, "Get 'em!"

④

Just Say Over, Over

"Let's get out of here!" I shouted. "The back door."

I rushed to the door holding my plastic nose and purple top hat. The rest of the gang followed. Felix was the last out, moving as fast as he could on the crutches. Darkness filled the alley and parking lot. Good thing. We needed to hide—and fast.

Orville and his friend rounded the building at the end of the alley.

We scattered. Sam ducked between two buildings. Megan followed. I hurried behind a brown van, then peeked around the rusty bumper.

Everyone had escaped ... except Felix.

"No fair," he told them. "I'm injured."

Orville grabbed Felix by the arm. "Too bad for you, Hop-along. Now move it." They walked on each side of him in the direction of church.

"That's weak!" Sam yelled. She emerged from between two buildings not far from Orville and the other SP. "Try catching someone who isn't hurt." She waved her hands in the air and dared them to come after her. "Chicken! Bawk. Bawk-bawk."

Orville ignored her. He knew Sam was trying to lure them away so Felix could escape. He also knew how fast Sam could run. They escorted Felix to the end of the alley and turned down the sidewalk.

We came together as a group and trailed them all the way to the church. Orville and the other SP took Felix to the roped-off area in the center of the play-ground. The Pen. Five other captured kids milled around with hands in pockets.

We watched from behind some bushes. Four Secret Police guarded the captives.

Mitch offered to go first. "I'll distract the guards. Then Sam can tag Felix."

"What's the point?" Crusher said. "Patterson ain't going anywhere."

He was right. Whatever diversion we used would have to distract the guards for a long time. A long long time. We sat on the grass behind the bushes and talked about what to do. Suddenly we realized that maybe the distraction wasn't dependent on us. Three kids from another team rushed the Pen. Two guards chased them off, but that left a side open. Sam didn't wait. She sprinted in and tagged Felix.

Chet jumped up and raised his arms like it was Superbowl Sunday. "The IQs never lose!"

When the guards came around, Mitch rushed in to create a diversion. Then kids from another team charged the Pen. The guards didn't know who to chase. They even bumped into each other. A kid high-fived a captive teammate and set him free. A dark-haired girl made a quick tag on a tall boy and he sprinted to freedom.

Chet flipped at that—literally.

Pretty soon the Pen was empty and everyone was rushing away with their teams.

Except Felix.

Even with all the distractions, the guards got to him before he could hide.

Sam and Mitch returned to us, breathing hard.

"You did what you could," Chet said. Even he sounded defeated.

Felix was the only one left in the Pen. He leaned on his crutches and glanced in our direction. I could tell he didn't want to give away our location, but he wanted to be with us more than anything. When Chet offered to talk to Joe about Felix, I told him no way. Of course Joe would allow Felix to hang out in the church until the game ended, but then he would miss out on everything.

Megan let out a sigh. "Then what can we do?"

"I'll hold them down until Patterson gets away," Crusher said.

That sounded just like Crusher. As the town bully, he had his own way of solving things. With force. He was probably the last guy on earth you'd expect to see at a church event. But here he was. For most of the year I avoided him at all costs. Then I took the blame for something that happened at school. After that he wasn't mean to me. That's when I realized even Crusher could change.

We were still debating over what to do when we heard a crackling sound. It came from my pocket. In all the commotion, I forgot that Felix and I had brought along walkie-talkies.

"Come in IQs," Felix said. "Over."

I squeezed the button on the side. "I can hear you, Felix."

Felix came right back at me. "Say, *over* when you're over. Over."

"Say over-over?" I asked, playing dumb.

"Not over-over. Just over. Over."

I grinned. "You did it again."

"Would you knock it off," Felix said. "Over."

"Okay. Okay. Hang on, Dude. We'll figure something out." I passed the walkie-talkie around. The IQs each took turns encouraging Felix.

But that wasn't enough.

"Forget it," Felix said. "Just go on without me. The rules allow for it. Over."

"No way," I said, determined not to desert my friend. "That's a negative. Over."

"I think we should listen to Felix," Chet said. "The rules say we can finish with a partial team. They add 10 minutes to our time for each team member in the Pen when we turn in our objects."

Mitch clarified what he heard. "That means if we finish first with Felix in the Pen, and the second team comes in five minutes later, they're the winners."

"You got it," Chet said. "But with Felix's injury, they probably won't give us the penalty."

"Just go," Felix said again. "I can't run. You'll never finish with me. Over."

"No way," Sam said, taking my side. "This is Felix's big night. We can't leave him."

"I can still help with the clues," Felix said. "I can keep you updated on the SPs too. Over."

"Forget it, Felix," I told him. "We're not leaving without you. Over and out." I stared at Felix alone in the Pen. He was the best friend I had. I would go to the ends of the earth for him. Lay down my life. He gave me another wave.

"Just go, Dude," Felix said. "I'll be all right. I've still got my backpack. I'll help you from here. Over."

I knew Felix was right. He couldn't run. Without him, we stood a chance. With him, it would take a miracle. I felt empty but there was no choice. Megan gave me a tug. I sighed and jogged away with my team into the night.

～～～

We made better time without Felix. Way better. The paint store turned out to be the right location for clue two and I ended up with a green and yellow

polka-dot bow tie. From there we sprinted to the
sporting goods store. Mitch felt certain that clue four,
Hole in one, had to be there. He marched inside and
approached the guy in the golf department.

Mitch snapped his fingers while he spoke. "Iggy,
Iggy, Iggy, have you seen my piggy?"

"You're in the wrong place, so stop bugging me,"
the guy replied. He bent over his putter and tapped the
ball. "Don't feel bad. You're the third group tonight.
See ya."

We gathered on the sidewalk.

"Bummer," Mitch said. "Where else could it be?"

Suddenly Crusher grabbed the sheet. "Gimme that
for a second." He held the paper toward the street
lamp so he could read it. "I think I know."

"You know?" Megan asked in surprise.

"What's that supposed to mean?" Crusher
demanded.

Megan just shrugged and looked down. I could tell
she felt bad. But we were probably all thinking the
same thing. I didn't think Crusher was smart enough
to solve the clues. Or that he cared enough to try. But
God was answering my prayers. Crusher wasn't just
staying. He was getting involved.

I stood up for Crusher. "Tell us where to go."

He didn't. He just took off down the sidewalk
without waiting for us to follow.

A Dark Chocolate Donut

Crusher thundered around the corner. We caught up with him just as he stopped in front of the donut shop.

"Of course," I said, getting it. *"A hole in one."*

Megan patted Crusher on the back. "Way to go."

Chet jumped around and tried to give Crusher a hug.

Crusher stepped back. "Don't push it."

I encouraged Crusher to go inside and say the rhyme.

"No way," Crusher said. "I found it. You do the rest."

Sam took my side. "Just finish the job, Leonard."

"Forget it. I'm not making a fool of myself."

"Who says you'll make a fool of yourself?" I questioned. "You say the rhyme and they answer. Easy as pie. I'm the one making a fool of myself."

"Willie's right," Sam added. "Just look at him."

"Total fool," Mitch said.

Everyone seemed a little too quick to agree that I was making a fool of myself.

"Freak city," Chet said.

Crusher looked at me and laughed. "That's for sure." He checked up and down the street. It was deserted. After muttering how nothing better go wrong, he pushed through the glass door. We crowded in behind him. The smell of fresh dough and chocolate filled the air. At first I thought Crusher would back down. Then his eyes locked on the tray of jelly donuts.

"Those look fresh," I quickly told him. "They're probably for whoever says the rhyme."

Crusher's eyes doubled in size. "You think?"

I prodded him. "Two words: Jelly. Donut."

He mumbled over the list of clues for a moment. "Wait a second. This rhyme's different."

I checked the sheet. He was right. "So? You can still do it."

"Can I help you?" a man with a white apron asked. He waited behind the counter and clapped flour from his hands.

Crusher took a last look at the clue sheet, then cleared his throat. "What do you say to the nitty gritty?"

The man smiled real big and leaned on the glass counter. "You don't get the prize 'til you sing me a ditty."

Crusher looked at the paper. "Yes! I was right."

"How 'bout, 'I'm a Little Tea Pot'?" the man asked him.

"Huh?" Crusher muttered, confused.

"You have to sing a ditty," Mitch whispered.

I kept my mouth shut.

"'I'm a Little Tea Pot'," Megan said. "You know." She quickly demonstrated the hand motions.

Crusher thought for a moment. The song must have registered. "No way. Forget it!" He glared at me. "You're toast, Plummet."

Sam stepped up and patted Crusher's shoulder. "You'll do great. Just go for it. Short and sweet."

"You mean, short and stout," Megan corrected her. The girls giggled and exchanged a wink.

I thought Crusher would pick me up and hurl me through the window. Or run outside and keep going. But he didn't. He tensed his jaw and let out a long breath. Just as he opened his mouth, three high schoolers came in the donut shop, two girls and a guy. Crusher turned bright red. He stepped to me and grabbed my bow tie. "Say your prayers."

"I have been," I choked.

He let go and eased to the counter. He cleared his throat, took a deep breath, and began to sing. "I'm a little tea pot, short and stout. Here is my handle. Here is my spout ..."

I've never fought so hard to keep a straight face. Here was the toughest kid in Glenfield Middle School, maybe the whole town, singing 'I'm a Little Tea Pot.' His voice sounded raspy, but not that bad. Something told me this wasn't just for a jelly donut. Maybe Crusher really wanted to win. And more than that, maybe he wanted to be a part of what we had in our youth group.

Crusher leaned sideways as he finished the song. "Just tip me over and pour me out."

Everyone clapped, even the high schoolers.

"Bravo! Bravo!" Megan and Sam chanted.

"Thank you. Thank you very much," Crusher said. He took a bow. "I'll be here all week. Tell your friends."

"I'm impressed," the man said. He turned around and lifted a fresh jelly donut from the rack. "This wasn't part of the deal, but have one on me."

"Awesome," Crusher said. "This church stuff ain't so bad." He ate the donut in two bites.

I pushed through the group for the counter. I didn't eat much dinner and was starting to feel hungry. "Um ... I'm the Clue Catcher, the guy who wears all the prizes."

The man eyed me with a smirk. "You sure?"

"Yeah. The glasses, bow tie—"

"I'm kidding," the man said, raising his hands. "I sort of figured it out. Wait here. I have a special donut for you, too."

"Score," I said. I turned and faced the group. "Chow time."

Suddenly everyone started to laugh. I turned back toward the counter.

The man stood there with an inner tube. "We call this our dark chocolate donut."

Mitch slid his finger across the tube then brought it to his mouth. "Mmm ... that's good. You scored."

The inner tube had two straps attached so it would hang on my shoulders. "But-but-"

"Bummer, Dude," Crusher laughed. He put the inner tube on me and gave me a bump. I bounced into the wall and right back.

"Cool," Mitch said. He shoved me too. I bounced over to Chet who bumped me toward Megan. She bounced me with her hip. I felt like a human bumper car. My purple top hat ended up on the ground. So did my fake nose and glasses. Something told me I would be next.

Good thing the static from the walkie-talkie caught everyone's attention.

"It must be Felix," Sam said. "Let's go."

We ran outside and down the street to get within range of the signal. We gathered in a dark area of an empty lot. Sam squeezed the talk button on the walkie-talkie. "Felix? Are you there? Over."

"Elix-Fay to oup-gray," came the reply. "Ome-cay in-ay. Over-ay."

"Huh?" Crusher wondered. "Now it's worse."

I told Crusher that Felix was using pig Latin. "You move the first consonant of a word to the back and add *ay*." I grabbed the walkie-talkie from Sam. "Knock it off. We're wasting time."

"Touchy!" Felix teased. "What's wrong with you?"

Sam took the walkie-talkie back. "He has to wear an inner tube around his waist. You should see him."

"I ish-way I ould-cay," Felix said. "Over."

Sam took my side on the pig Latin and Felix reluctantly agreed to knock it off. He even quit saying "over." But he acted really sad about it, like he was giving up on the whole thing. He told us that more kids had been captured from other groups, but were soon freed. In talking with them, he had learned how many clues their teams had solved. "Five for one, four for the other."

"Tell Patterson we're up to four," Crusher said. "And who pulled it off."

Sam filled him in.

"I wish I could have been there," Felix said. "Anyway, you guys better hurry. They just sent two Pen guards out to catch people."

"Only two guards are left with you?" I asked.

Felix read my mind. "Don't try it, Dude. They're too fast. I'd never make it."

"Crusher could hold two guards down," I said.

Crusher flexed his arm and said, "The beach is that way."

Felix told us to not worry about him. He was still on our team and wanted to win. "Now get going and solve more clues—fast!"

We gathered around and had another look at the clue sheet. Mitch read number five aloud. *"Classic birds of thunder near mint condition."* He made a fist and knocked his forehead. "I've seen this one. But where?" He snapped his fingers. "That's it!" He took off. Everyone sprinted after him. The inner tube bounced between my waist and armpits. I held the top hat and glasses. We kept in the dark parts of town, out of sight. Eventually we came to a car dealership. Another group ran away as we arrived.

We hurried to the giant windows.

"There it is," Mitch said. "A 1959 Ford Thunderbird. A classic in mint condition."

"Cool," I said.

We split up to find a way inside. We rushed from locked door to locked door. We pushed and knocked. No answer. No people.

"This has to be the right place," I said. I tried the door to the Parts Department. I shook it good and pushed.

Big mistake.

The alarm wailed. It sounded like a school bell—only louder.

Rinnng! Rinnng! Rinnng!

6

Prince Charming

Chet rushed up and pulled me from the door. "What'd you do? What'd you do?" His neck turned to rubber as he searched this way and that. He acted like the police would swoop down at any moment. "This is bad. Real bad."

I backed away from the door. "I tried the knob. That's it!"

A security guard in a blue uniform came out of nowhere. He had a flattop and no neck. He shined a flashlight in our faces and gave us an earful. We went on and on about how sorry we were. Eventually the security guard softened up. He even offered to take a look at the clue sheet. "I can see why you're here, but I can't help you. Maybe mint means candy."

"The candy store!" Megan said. "Maybe there's a Thunderbird parked next to it."

We thanked the security guard and rushed away.

We didn't find a Thunderbird near the candy store, but we went inside just in case.

Sam read from the sheet. "Iggy, Iggy, Iggy, have you seen my piggy?"

The girl at the counter sized us up. "Orky, Orky, Orky, yes I've seen your porky."

"Yes!" Sam said. "We got it." She jumped around. It made me feel better to see her having fun and not stressing so much over her testimony.

"Hold on," the girl said. "You with the tube, can you spin to win?"

"Sure," I said. "I turned in a complete circle."

"You can do better than that," the girl told me. "This is where the rubber meets the road."

I figured out what she meant and got down on the floor. I rolled in a complete circle.

"Spin to win," the girl said again.

Crusher and Mitch rolled me in circles as fast as they could. I spun all right.

"Roll! Roll!" the girls chanted.

When I finally stood up, my legs turned to noodles. My head kept spinning. I stumbled into Chet then Sam.

The candy store girls clapped with approval.

"Now I feel guilty," one said to the other.

"Huh?" I questioned.

She cringed and didn't look at me. "I went to the Lock-In three years ago."

"Five for me," the other added. "We're not part of this year's clues. We just wanted to have some fun with you."

I moaned and leaned on the counter.

The girl handed me a free sucker. "For being such a great sport."

Sam pointed at the sucker and patted my shoulder. "Kinda makes sense, huh?"

Everyone was still laughing when the other girl came over. "Here's another treat for you." She winked and handed me a chocolate coin wrapped in gold foil. "Near mint condition."

My eyes nearly popped out of my head. "Are we in the right place?"

The girl smiled. "Nope. Sorry."

I stared at the girl then back at the coin. My mind raced. I thought. Then it hit me. Like a ton of gold, it hit me.

"Come on," I said. "Hurry!"

I led the IQs down the street. Suddenly it all made sense. Mom and Dad working late. Phoebe helping them. I got it. I didn't stop until we were inside Plummet's Hobbies. I went straight to the register. My parents and Phoebe laughed at the sight of me, but I didn't care. I quoted the phrase and waited for their response.

Phoebe beamed. "Orky, Orky, Orky, yes, I've seen your porky."

"No tricks?" I asked my dad.

"No tricks," he said.

Phoebe reached under the counter and removed a red piece of clothing. "Custom long johns just for you. Extra large."

I slapped my forehead. "Don't tell me ..."

Phoebe nodded. "You have to put it on."

"But I'm already wearing an inner tube."

My mom said that the long johns were large enough to fit over the tube. I started to complain, then stopped myself. Why bother? I stepped into the red outfit while telling everyone how I solved the clue. "Our hobby store sells model Thunderbirds. Next door is Classic Coins."

"You're the man, Willie!" Chet cheered. He pointed at me with one hand then the other, back and forth.

"Well? How do I look?" I turned real slow, posing.

"Like a teenage Santa Claus," Sam said.

"Actually, I was thinking you look more like a young *Prince Charming*," Megan snickered.

Sam twisted me around so she could read my chest. "Or what about, *Cutie Pie.*"

I looked down and realized why everyone was laughing. Pink and white lettering covered the red material. *Cutie Pie* decorated the front. *Heart Throb* ran down one leg, *Hunk* down the other.

"No way. Forget it! I'm not wearing these." I started to unbutton them.

"Come on, Willie," Megan said. "They're cute."

"That's 'cause I painted them," Phoebe said. "And only Willie's." She stepped between me and Megan. "I wanted to paint a scene on the back where it says *Prince Charming*, but I ran out of time."

"Bummer," Crusher joked. "That would have been *so* special. Huh, Cutie?"

I glared at Crusher. The memories came rushing back. When I ran for class president, Phoebe painted a banner for me. It featured me in a suit of armor. Before I could stop her, she put the banner up in the cafeteria. I still had nightmares over that one. I kept at the buttons until Sam grabbed my fingers.

"Do it for Felix, Willie," Sam said. "Let's win this for him."

That got to me. I let out a sigh and reversed my fingers. I asked Sam to radio Felix. This time we were close enough to the church to hear him clearly.

"We got number five," Sam told him. "At Plummet's Hobbies." She explained what happened.

Suddenly Felix kicked into pig Latin. "Ixnay on the ocation-lay. Over."

"Not that again," I moaned.

"Get out of there!" Felix warned. "The guards heard you. They're coming! Hide!"

Phoebe hurried to the front window. She cupped her hands against the glass and looked up the street. She was quiet. But not for long. "I think that's them."

My dad ushered the IQs into the lab. I hurried after them, still going at the buttons on the long underwear. With the inner tube blocking my view, I didn't see the box of models. I tripped and creamed a glue display. Tubes went flying.

Phoebe came over and helped me up. "Flee thee quickly, my prince!"

"Knock that off," I told her.

Phoebe giggled and waved good-bye, as if she was a princess and I was going off to fight a dragon.

I crawled into the lab just as Mitch flung open the back door to the alley and started to leave.

"Wait a second!" I shouted. I explained that we should hide in the lab and leave the back door open. "They'll think we left."

We scattered to the nooks and dark areas of the room. Crusher huddled behind a box. Mitch headed for the bathroom. Chet slid under the workbench. I squeezed into the closet with Megan and Sam. With the inner tube around my waist we barely fit.

"Gimme some room, Jumbo," Sam teased.

She bumped me with her hip. I squished into Megan. She bumped me back.

"Stop—*hiccup*—it." I slapped my hand over my mouth. Of all the times to get the hiccups.

Shoes tromped into the hobby store.

"Back there," a guy said. He sounded big—tough. His voice had SP written all over it.

In no time they were in the lab. For some reason, their shoes stuck to the floor and peeled off with a screech.

"They went out the back," a nasally voice said. Screech. Screech. It sounded like tape being ripped up with each step.

"You sure?" the tough one asked.

The feet slowed down. Screech. Screech. "Stupid shoes."

The tough one answered. "Patterson did it. I bet you." Screech. Screech.

They grumbled back and forth. The nasally SP wanted to check around the lab, but the tough guy thought they should keep going.

They stood still. No screeching. No talking.

The hiccup took me by surprise. I tried to hold it in, but some got out.

"What was that?" nasal nose asked. His sticky shoes grew louder. Screech. Screech.

I heard my dad's voice. "Can I help you boys with something?"

Suddenly the SPs sounded timid. I think they realized they shouldn't be snooping around in someone's business. Good thing Orville wasn't with them.

"Um ... no. We were just leaving," the tough one said.

Their shoes screeched out the back door.

Sam pushed open the closet and checked to see if they were gone. They were.

"Great hiccup," Megan said sarcastically.

Sam agreed. "Where's Felix when we need him?"

I knew what she was getting at and told her no thanks. During the year I had a bad case of the hiccups. Felix came up with one crazy cure after another. "Remember when he put that hot sauce on my hamburger?"

"Yeah," Crusher said, coming over. "I ate it."

Just thinking about it made me laugh. Even Crusher grinned at the memory.

"Come on. We got to go," Chet said. "This is our night. Am I right?"

"You bet, Chet," Mitch answered.

Not me. I paused in the doorway of the closet, still thinking about Felix. So what if his inventions didn't always work out? He was my best friend. "We have to free Felix, you guys."

Chet objected. "There's no way."

"There has to be a way. He's an IQ. He'd do the same for us."

Megan added that Felix couldn't run and we would need the world's biggest distraction to get him out of the Pen. She was still talking when I saw it.

"Distraction, huh?" I pointed at the back corner of the lab. "If the Skyrunner 1000 can distract the whole town, what's a few SPs?"

No one argued with me. But they wondered how we would win if we had to wait for Felix to get around on crutches.

I shrugged. "We'll figure something out. I'd rather free Felix than win anyway."

"Me too," Sam admitted. "But you're forgetting one small detail. The Skyrunner 1000 needs helium balloons to fly."

Megan spoke up. "I saw some in the youth room at the start of the Lock-In."

"That's SP headquarters," Mitch protested.

I thought for a moment then came up with an idea. The IQs thought it had potential. Mitch and Crusher picked up the Skyrunner 1000 and brought it along. To make sure we avoided the SPs, we left through the front of the store.

"Bye, my brave Prince Charming," Phoebe said. She patted my inner tube belly. "Watch thy step."

The IQs cracked up.

"Why me?" I whined, squeezing through the door.

I hid in a cluster of bushes where I could keep an eye on Felix and the youth room at the same time. My plan was simple. Chet and Mitch would distract the Secret Police. Sam and Crusher would sneak in and grab some helium balloons. Megan waited with me in case something went wrong. The Skyrunner 1000 was stored safely at the launch pad.

Mitch crouched near the youth room. When I gave him thumbs up, he tapped on the window and taunted the high schoolers inside. "Anyone know where I can find some Secret Police?"

Two SPs rushed outside and chased after Mitch. Chet pulled the same stunt and more followed. Sam and Crusher took the cue and sprinted for the room. Getting in would be easy. Getting out would be another story. Suddenly, Sam appeared. She had a fistful of strings with balloons. Crusher must have sacrificed himself so she could get free.

My heart raced. The plan had worked!

Or had it? An SP came out of nowhere. Sam cut to the left and dodged him. He kept coming. She hurdled a fire hydrant. So did he. The balloons trailed behind her. She skidded in the grass. The SP pounced. Sam's hand opened and the balloons floated away.

"No," I moaned. I dropped my head. Defeat.

"Look!" Megan said.

Crusher burst from the youth room. He didn't have more balloons. He had a tank. A helium tank. It had to weigh 80 pounds. Crusher carried it under his arm like a football. By the time the SPs saw him, he was out of range.

"Get back here!" one shouted.

Crusher didn't slow down and the SPs didn't try to catch him. They probably figured why bother? Crusher was fast, strong, and gone.

Within a few minutes Mitch and Chet joined us in the bushes. From there we headed to a hill in the park near the church. The Skyrunner 1000 was there, waiting for us. So was Crusher.

Chet stared. "You brought the tank?"

Crusher shrugged. "Had to. All the filled balloons were gone." He pulled a handful of empty balloons from his pocket. Chet told us that as soon as we finished we were taking the tank back. Everyone agreed. We just wanted to launch the Skyrunner 1000. Megan started filling balloons while I told the guys about Crusher's incredible run. They gave him pats on the back. Crusher acted like it was no big deal, but I could tell the compliments meant a lot to him.

Mitch reminded us that Sam needed to be rescued too.

"Believe me," I said. "There's no bigger distraction than the Skyrunner 1000."

Megan filled another balloon and gave it to me. I tied it to the Skyrunner 1000. "Better do a few more. These balloons are smaller than the silver ones we used before."

"Way to go, Leonard," Megan teased. "You brought us dinky balloons."

Crusher grabbed the red balloon she was filling and put it to his mouth. He inhaled deeply from the helium. "Excuse me!" he squeaked. He sounded like a Munchkin.

Everyone cracked up. Who would have thought such a mean kid could be so much fun? Graduating from eighth grade probably had a lot to do with it. But I hoped that it was more than that, that God was doing something in Crusher's life.

"Is this better?" Megan asked. The orange balloon looked like it would pop.

"I guess," I shrugged. "Still seems small."

"Excuuuuuuse meeeeee," Crusher squeaked.

I finished tying on the assortment of rainbow colored balloons. They seemed way too full, but we needed all the lifting power we could get.

"Skyrunner 1000?" Crusher joked. "Looks more like the Spaceship Lollipop."

At that Mitch took a breath of helium and sang out, "On the space ... ship, lol-li-pop."

Crusher inhaled some helium and joined him.

Suddenly the mighty IQs sounded like Munchkins on parade.

"No more goofing off," Chet said. "We've got teammates to rescue."

Mitch squeaked. "You bet, Chet!"

Crusher pulled a Munchkin too. "No sweat, Chet."

"Don't fret, Chet," Mitch added.

While they kept at it, I gave the rope a quick pull to start the engine. Nothing. I yanked it again. The motor sputtered. On the third pull, it popped, then started up. I gave it some gas. The main propeller and smaller back propellers spun faster and faster.

"Here we go!" I worked the remote. The Skyrunner 1000 lifted off the ground. The wind from the propellers blew the purple top hat from my head. I adjusted the controls. The Skyrunner 1000 turned in a big circle, floating higher and higher.

"That's awesome," Mitch said.

Megan's mouth fell open. "Amazing."

"You made that?" Chet asked.

I grinned and nodded. It was neat to hear their compliments, but even cooler to see the Skyrunner 1000 flying again. I steered it through a figure eight, then veered toward church.

Time to free our friends.

Time for a little invasion from Planet X.

A Wild Pack

We hurried to a spot where we could see the Pen. Felix and Sam stood near the rope. A few other kids waited with them. The noise from the Skyrunner 1000 caught their attention. But the darkness hid it from view.

Suddenly, Felix came on the radio. "IQs are you there? What's that sound?"

I squeezed the walkie-talkie with one hand and the remote with the other. "You don't recognize it?"

Sam came on next. "Don't tell me it's the—"

"Affirmative," I replied. I cut her off so she would-n't spill the beans. We couldn't take any chances that an SP might hear. Chet took the walkie-talkie. I focused on playing pilot.

"Let's do it!" I shouted. I angled the Skyrunner 1000 straight for the Pen. The lights from the church parking lot lit up the sky. The balloons came into view. Everyone froze. The Secret Police stared with wide eyes, their heads doubled back. The kids in the Pen did too. Felix and Sam shouted and exchanged a high five. I think they were just as proud as I was to see the Skyrunner 1000 flying again.

"Now," Chet ordered. "Go!"

Crusher headed for the youth room with the helium tank. Mitch sprinted for the Pen. The Skyrunner 1000 spun a tight circle then rocked to the side. Mitch ran up and tagged Sam. A minute later Crusher arrived and slapped hands with Felix. The guards stared at the sky, spell-bound.

All except one. Orville.

"Hey, get back here!" he shouted.

Felix ducked under the rope and hopped away on his crutches. Orville rushed out from the buildings. Sam escaped, but Felix didn't stand a chance. Orville grabbed him and brought him back to the Pen. Orville also got on the SPs for being so distracted. Everyone but Felix was free.

They ignored Orville and watched the Skyrunner 1000 climb higher and higher. Pretty soon it would be out of sight.

"Bring it back down," Megan said. "We need to try again."

As Sam ran up, she answered for me. "He can't. Remember, Willie?"

That's when it hit me. We had to pop the balloons to get the Skyrunner 1000 to land. "Anyone have a pellet gun handy?" I asked sheepishly.

We watched the Skyrunner 1000 rise into the night. Crusher made another attempt at Felix, but failed. He rejoined us just as the Skyrunner 1000 vanished. We needed a miracle—and fast.

I told Chet to get on the radio. "Tell Felix I'm sorry."

"You can't," Sam replied. "I have his walkie-talkie."

So much for operation rescue. The whir of the Skyrunner 1000 engine faded above us.

Softer. Softer.

Pop!

"What was that?" I asked. The engine grew louder.

Pop!

The Skyrunner 1000 eased into view, minus the two balloons that had popped.

"Now aren't you glad I overfilled the balloons?" Megan said.

I was about to say yes when another balloon popped.

"It's coming at us," an SP warned. They started to scatter.

Crusher didn't waste any time. He sprinted full speed for Felix. Orville was waiting. That did it. He was about to learn what an inventive little brother could do. I steered the Skyrunner 1000 toward Orville.

"Hit the dirt!" Orville yelled. He dove on the grass as the Skyrunner 1000 zipped over his head. Then he

crawled full speed for a building. Crusher rushed to
the Pen and put Felix on his back. They took off with
Felix wearing his backpack and squeezing his crutches under his arm. They charged across the parking lot.

Felix whooped and hollered. "Charge!"

No one followed. Felix and Crusher could have
taken their own sweet time. We welcomed them with
handshakes and cheers. The mighty IQs were together again.

"Can I have a try?" Felix asked, reaching for the
remote. He balanced on one foot.

"You sure?" I asked. "You seem—"

"I'm fine," Felix said, cutting me off. He grabbed
the remote and started getting fancy. At first he did
great. Then he lost balance. He waved his arms and
fell. The remote smacked the ground.

"Uh-oh," Felix said.

The Skyrunner 1000 wheeled out of control. Felix
worked the controls. He tried to steer up. Go sideways. Nothing. It wouldn't respond. Good thing everyone had gone inside. My greatest invention veered
and leaned. The propellers trimmed a tree. It dove
again, this time faster than ever. Felix smacked the
remote with his knuckles. That did something. The
tail propellers gave enough lift for a stall at about 10
feet. After that the Skyrunner 1000 dropped like a
stone. Not on the ground. Not on the parking lot. Not
in the grass. But in the back of Orville's truck.

"At least no one got hurt," Felix said.

"Not yet," I moaned, thinking about what Orville would do to me. "Not yet."

We took a few minutes before moving on. Felix updated us on everything he had learned while in the Pen. Only one group had six clues solved. The rest were at five like us.

"Then what are we waiting for?" Megan said. We gathered around the sheet and studied the final two clues.

"How long do we have?" Mitch asked.

Chet rolled his wrist and checked. "Thirty minutes."

"Really?" Sam asked. Her face dropped. "That means 30 minutes until my testimony."

I told her there would be other stuff like singing, devotions, and prayer before her faith story, but that didn't help.

"Prayer, huh?" Crusher mumbled. He looked more concerned than Sam.

Chet noticed. He tried to fire us up. "Come on IQs. Let's win this! Are you with me?"

"You bet, Chet!" Felix shouted. Then cupped his hand over my ear and whispered. "I never thought I'd be glad to say that again."

Crusher frowned and kicked the dirt. "Don't kid yourself. With Hop-along and Hippo-boy, we don't stand a chance."

Felix patted the inner tube around my waist. "How's it going, Hippo-boy?"

"Can somebody remind me why we helped Felix escape?" I asked the group.

Felix smiled. "I'll tell you why. I just solved number five. Let's go."

Carrying Felix piggyback seemed like the fastest way to travel. Mitch started off. Chet followed. Then came my turn to carry him.

"This inner tube makes a great seat," Felix said.

"Don't get too comfortable up there," I told him. "These long johns make me sweat." I took lots of short breaths and forced myself to keep running.

Felix directed us to Tina's Restaurant. The hostess didn't even let Mitch finish the rhyme before sending him back outside.

Felix defended his conclusion. *"Flame boiled. Grade A. Traditional seating.* It has to be a restaurant."

We agreed and tried another one. And another. Eventually, I wasn't the only one sweating from carrying Felix. But I was the only one getting laughed at. You'd think people had never seen a kid wearing a fake nose and glasses, a purple top hat, a yellow and green bow tie, and inflated, red long underwear before.

"We're narrowing it down," Felix told us.

"Can we narrow a little faster?" Mitch asked on his second time around with Felix. "Hop-along weighs a ton."

"I heard that," Felix said.

"We need something for you to ride," Chet suggested. "Like a bike."

"I can't peddle with one foot," Felix complained.

"We need a wagon, or something we can pull him in," Megan said.

"That's it!" I exclaimed. "The Sidewalk Dogsled!" I explained my plan but no one liked it. They didn't think we had time to round up the dogs.

"Who needs dogs?" I said. "We've got us."

"Are you calling me a dog?" Megan asked.

"No!" I said, shaking my head. "I wouldn't do that—ever! I just meant we can pull the dogsled and Felix can steer. It's perfect—and fast!"

Everyone agreed to give it a try. We rushed to my house, trading Felix on the way. While I dug the Sidewalk Dogsled from the garage, Crusher drank from the hose and let out a howl.

Sam bit her lip and spoke to Megan. "This is getting scary."

I put a pillow on the Sidewalk Dogsled to make it more comfortable for Felix. The dogsled consisted of an old Soapbox Derby cart and some two-by-fours. The wheels were fast and sturdy. I grabbed some rope and we were ready to go.

Felix beamed when he sat down. "You're the man, Willie."

"Actually, he's the dog," Sam said.

Crusher wanted to know why I built the cart in the first place.

"It started with the Monopoly game we were playing," I explained. "From there I learned some real life business lessons." It told him how I combined my dog-walking business with my job at Sir Quick printers.

We moved down the driveway to the sidewalk. Mitch and Chet were in the front, followed by Megan and Sam. Crusher and I followed them. Felix held the ropes that I had used to steer the dogs. I told him to go easy on us.

"Are you kidding? A wild pack like you?" Felix's smile doubled the size of his face. He was loving this, I could tell. "What are you waiting for? Mush! MUSH!"

A Runaway Sidewalk Dogsled

We got pretty good at pulling Felix. It just took a few blocks. We started with a jog, then kicked into a run. With six of us pulling, we made good time. Felix took a few spills before learning how to steer. But then he got it down. He even managed to keep an eye on the clue sheet.

"That's it!" he exclaimed, thinking he had solved another clue. "Mush! Mush! Faster! To the school."

"Huh?" I asked in disbelief.

"Not school," Crusher complained.

Chet tried to cheer us on. But he couldn't get a *You bet, Chet* to save his life. Getting this far through junior high was hard enough. The last thing we wanted was to go there now.

"Mush!" Felix shouted. He flipped the ropes to keep us going. Sam convinced us to turn down her street. She said it was faster. But I knew the real reason. She wanted to see if her dad's car was in the driveway.

It wasn't.

After a few more blocks, we jogged across the parking lot. A few parking spaces still had cars in them. I hoped none belonged to my teachers. One look at me and they'd laugh into the next school year.

We parked the Sidewalk Dogsled and Felix climbed on Crusher's back. The door to the main entry was open. We rushed inside. Our shoes echoed down the empty hall. It felt weird to be at school without lockers slamming or kids talking. Creepy even.

"My locker," Mitch said. He paused to spin the dial. "It hasn't changed a bit."

"That's because it's only been five hours since you saw it," Megan said dryly.

Hearing that seemed strange. It already felt longer. Maybe that's why we all started to reminisce.

"The good old cafeteria," Sam said. She grinned at Megan. "I can practically still see Phoebe's poster of Willie running for class president."

I knew she was teasing me, so I threw out a zinger of my own. "Can you? Because I can still see you wearing that dress to impress your secret admirer." I glanced at Crusher.

Sam slugged me in the arm. Crusher had turned out to be her secret admirer. When Sam found out, she nearly died of embarrassment.

"What about when Felix put hot sauce on your hamburger to cure your hiccups?" Megan said.

"I wanted to pulverize him," I said.

"Me too," Crusher added.

"You wanted to pulverize everyone," Felix said to Crusher.

"He did pulverize everyone," I said.

Crusher patted my back. "Thanks for noticing."

"Except Ernie Pignatello," Felix reminded us. He told Chet about when Ernie took a swing at Crusher and how Crusher ended up on the floor with a bloody mouth. "Ernie was one of the smallest kids in school."

Chet didn't believe Felix.

"It's true," Felix said. "Ask Willie."

Chet looked at me.

I explained that the blood was really ketchup.

"I thought it tasted kind of sweet," Crusher said.

We relived a few more memories. The more we talked, the more recent and real they became. Like our whole lives began and ended at Glenfield Middle School.

We hurried past Miss Pell's English class and Mrs. McNelly's drama class.

That's when I knew where we were going. "Don't tell me, Mr. Keefer."

Felix nodded and explained. *"Flame boiled* tipped me off. Meat is flame *broiled*, not boiled. Mr. Keefer loved to boil chemicals over the Bunsen burner. *Grade A* totally fits school. So does *traditional seating*. We always sat in rows."

We tromped down the hall and turned the corner. Mr. Keefer's open door welcomed us. He waited at the front of the classroom, conducting an experiment with some beakers and test tubes. Brown and gray stains blotted his white lab coat. He was so into his project, he didn't even notice my goofy costume.

"Have a seat," he said as we stopped in front of him. "You're late."

Felix flashed an *I told you so* grin at the IQs. Then he spoke up. "Iggy, Iggy, Iggy, have you seen my piggy?"

Mr. Keefer looked up. "Excuse me?"

Felix swallowed and repeated himself. His confident grin vanished.

"As a matter of fact," Mr. Keefer said. "Orky, Orky, Orky, yes I've seen your porky."

Celebration time. We jumped around and cheered. I gave Megan a bump with my inner tube hip, then went after Sam. Once we all calmed down, Mr. Keefer handed me a beaker full of a bubbling gray liquid.

I tried to hand it back, but he wouldn't take it. That made me nervous. So much for celebration time. Mr. Keefer's experiments had a way of sounding alarms and causing evacuations.

"What am I supposed to do with it?" I asked. It was pretty obvious I couldn't wear it.

"Drink it," Mr. Keefer told me.

I eyed the gray bubbling stuff and made a face. Crusher reminded me that he had to sing, 'I'm a Little Teapot.' When I still refused, he threatened to stuff me in a teapot. That made the difference. I took a little sip. Fuzzy. Cold. Yuk.

Suddenly Felix grabbed my shoulder. "Get down."

We dropped to the floor.

"I think I saw an SP," Felix warned.

We kept low and quiet. Soon we heard screeching on the hall floor.

"That's them," Felix told us. "When I was in the Pen, I put adhesive on the guard's shoes. Guzzle. Quick!"

I gulped down the drink. Sam hurried to lock the door.

The drink froze my throat. The fizz burned. Then the pain traveled to my head. "Brain freeze!"

Sam rushed back and had us stand. "It's okay. No one was there."

"I guess it just sounded like them," Felix admitted. He slapped my back. "So how was that drink?"

"BURP!" I erupted. Thanks to Felix I went from brain freeze to burp ease in one gulp!

Mr. Keefer explained that he was perfecting a new smoothie that combined raisins and root beer. "The other Clue Catchers just took a sip."

"Oops," Felix laughed.

"I'll show you—*BURRRP*—oops," I told him.

I've never seen a one-legged-Felix move so fast. He hopped like a bullfrog and I sounded like one.

I chased Felix around and everyone laughed. Mr. Keefer started to tell us to stop, then changed his tone. He said how much he would miss us. Felix and I stopped running around. We told Mr. Keefer we would miss him too. His experiments didn't always come out just right, but his class was never boring. And we really did learn a lot about science. It occurred to me that maybe one of the reasons Felix and I were so into inventing was because of Mr. Keefer. I told him so.

He didn't say much, but he blinked a lot and rubbed his eyes. I could tell he was grateful.

Chet mentioned that we should get going and Mr. Keefer took the hint. He reached into his desk and removed two kneepads painted with zebra stripes.

I put them on and strutted back and forth as if I was a model on a catwalk. The IQs cheered me on. I stood for a moment feeling good. Six clues down and two to go. We were almost there.

Then a scary face flattened against the outside window.

The SPs had found us.

⁓⁓⁓

Good thing the outside door to Mr. Keefer's class was locked. The SPs had to run around the building and come down the hall like we did. That gave us time to plan our escape. Once it was clear, Mr. Keefer unlocked the outside door. Mitch carried Felix as we hurried toward the Sidewalk Dogsled. With Felix on his pillow, we grabbed the ropes and ran down the darkest street we could find.

But it wasn't dark enough. As we crested the hill, the SPs rushed from the school.

"They're coming," I said. "Faster!"

"Mush!" Felix ordered.

The hill worked to our advantage ... at first. We sprinted full speed. Then we learned an important lesson. Wheels go faster down hills than feet. The Sidewalk Dogsled nipped at our heels.

"More mush!" Felix cried.

Everyone kicked it up a notch. Except me. Running with an inner tube around my waist wasn't the best thing for speed. I tripped and rolled across someone's yard. As I looked up, Sam and Megan lunged out of the way. Mitch and Chet followed. Crusher hung in there the longest. But eventually the dogsled knocked his feet out from under him. We watched in horror as Felix sped down the hill.

"Ahhhh!" Felix wailed.

A steep turn at the bottom waited for him. Wheels skidded and Felix leaned. But he couldn't dodge the curb. The Sidewalk Dogsled smashed into the concrete and splintered into pieces. Felix launched into a big green hedge. And disappeared.

The IQs sprinted to help him.

I pulled the branches apart. "Are you okay in there, Felix?"

I poked my head into the bushes. So did Sam.

Felix held his injured ankle. "That hurt."

We were still figuring out what to do when Chet sounded a warning. "SPs!"

Everyone scattered. Sam squeezed into the hedge with Felix. I tried, but couldn't fit and had to settle for an old car in a nearby driveway. I hid behind the bumper and waited. Screechy feet tromped by but didn't stop.

After a while, Sam ventured out. I joined her, and we helped Felix to his feet. He slung his backpack over his shoulder.

We called for the rest of the IQs, but no one answered. We called again. Silence.

The rest of our team was gone.

Splits City

With the Sidewalk Dogsled smashed to pieces, Sam and I decided to support Felix between us. He leaned on our shoulders and limped. We were too tired to carry him piggyback. Since I had the inner tube around me, Sam bore most of the weight. We tried to figure out what happened to the rest of the IQs. Captured by SPs or still running made the most sense.

"Why am *I* always the one bailing you guys out?" she asked.

"No, you're not," Felix said.

"Gimme a break," Sam shot back. "What about the poacher with the spear gun? Who rowed us to safety?"

"Okay, once," I conceded.

Sam wasn't finished. "What about when your automatic ice cream scooper went bonkers in the

Founders' Day Parade? Whose flag team distracted the crowds until you got things sorted out?"

"Okay, twice." I admitted. "But don't forget the time I saved you from that giant tidal wave at the water park."

Sam agreed but reminded me that she was the one who stopped the Classic Coins burglar with a perfect throw.

"Yeah, but who untied Felix?" I added.

"I guess I owe you both some thanks," Felix said. "Just like now."

We talked and relived memories. We kept thinking we would come across some of the IQs, but didn't. Felix tried his walkie-talkie, but the other one went off in Sam's pocket.

"This is Am-Say," Sam replied. She squeezed the button on the handset and held the walkie-talkie to her mouth. "State your location, Elix-fay. Over."

"Real funny," Felix moaned.

We decided to head back to the church. The shortest way there was through the back parking lot of an old apartment complex. Red and gray graffiti covered a section of wall. Weeds pushed through the cracked blacktop. A few cars rested on cement blocks.

Halfway through, two guys stepped out from behind a brown van. They moved in front of us. The taller guy stretched his fingers then brought them into a fist. Green tattoos covered his forearm.

"What do you want?" the heavy one demanded. His dirty shirt had a rip down the side.

We took a few more steps then stopped.

The tall one punched his hand. "Look at this, a limp and a blimp."

I tried to keep things friendly, so I laughed. I told them we were on a church event and just cutting through.

"No, you're not," the big guy with the ripped shirt told me. Oil stains dotted his jeans. "Not unless we say so." He read some of the names on my red long johns and made jokes about how stupid I looked. *"Cutie Pie?* Sure."

I glanced at Felix then Sam. "I guess we can go around."

The tall one shook his head then spit. "How much you got?"

"Huh?" Felix asked.

"Money," the big guy grunted. He stared at me. "How much?"

I didn't tell him. Felix and Sam didn't either. The three of us squeezed together. My heart pounded.

The heavy guy moved behind us. The tall guy extended his hand. "I said how much? Let's see it."

"We'll just go around," Sam said. "No big deal."

"No big deal," the heavy guy mimicked.

The tall one laughed then narrowed his eyes. "Money. Now!"

I felt my knees shaking. I prayed through trembling lips. I couldn't believe we were being forced to hand over our money. But if we didn't, what would they do? They were bigger than us and older. Felix reached into his pocket. I looked around, wishing officer Sutton was near. He wasn't.

"Hurry up," the heavy guy said. He gave me a shove.

I steadied myself to keep from falling.

"You heard 'em. Hurry up," a voice ordered from out of nowhere.

"Huh?" the tall guy grumbled, looking around.

Crusher appeared between two of the apartment buildings. "You heard them. Hurry up."

"I thought it was you, Grubb," the taller one said. He must have expected Crusher to help them because he talked about how we wouldn't pay.

"Why should they?" Crusher demanded. "They're with me."

The heavy guy looked at Crusher like he was crazy. "They said they're on a church event."

"So?" Crusher told them about the Lock-In. He tried to make it sound cool. He covered the highlights, talking about the pizza, games, and cute girls. That didn't matter. The thugs ridiculed him anyway. They asked him if he forgot his Bible. He shrugged it off and took Sam's place under Felix's arm. The guys poured on the insults, but they didn't go after our money or try and stop us. They just laughed and told Crusher to have fun at church and be a good little boy.

We hurried from the darkness of the parking lot to the street.

"Thanks, Leonard," Sam said.

Felix and I thanked Crusher too. He just told us to forget about it and hurry up.

We crossed a few more streets and joined the rest of the IQs in the park. They had managed to hide there and avoid capture. They were glad to see us, but reality had set in. Only 15 minutes left and we still had two clues that needed solving.

"Maybe the other teams couldn't solve them either," Megan suggested.

"No chance," Felix said. He took another look at the clue sheet. It looked like he would cry. "I'm sorry about my ankle. You guys should have just left me in the Pen."

"Don't start that again," I said. Everyone backed me. Even Crusher.

"You could have solved them all without me," Felix went on. He glared at his ankle like it was his worst enemy. He put some weight on it but winced in pain.

I told him to quit focusing on himself and help us figure out another clue.

I read number eight aloud. *"A historic fish."*

Chet stroked his chin.

Megan rubbed her temples.

I took off my top hat to let my brain breathe. Anything to spark my thoughts. "Something tells me I know this place. It's just not clicking."

"It better click soon," Chet said. "If we get back late, we're automatically disqualified."

"A historic fish," Felix repeated. "We tried the pet store and the market. Where else do you find fish?"

"Maybe we should focus on *historic*," Sam said.

"Maybe we should work on clue seven," Crusher said.

I snapped my fingers. "No, wait. That's it! *A historic fish.* Get it?"

The IQs answered with blank faces.

"Colonel Pike's estate is Glenfield's only National Historic Landmark," I told them. "And a pike is a fish!"

"Ten minutes and counting," Chet warned. "Should we risk it?"

Every IQ answered at once. "YOU BET, CHET!"

I grabbed Felix's crutches and explained how we would make a stretcher. Chet and I would run in front. Crusher and Mitch would run in back. We'd hold the crutches on our shoulders. Felix would rest on top of them.

"Let's do it!" Felix shouted.

We stood up with Felix in place. We progressed from walk to jog to run. With four of us to share the load, we moved fast.

"You guys are kind of bumpy," Felix told us. "Can you smooth it out a little?"

Chet and I exchanged a glance then veered away from each other. That meant splits city for Felix.

"I was kidding! I was kidding!" he pleaded.

We moved back together and kept the pace. Three minutes later we arrived at Colonel Pike's. His house was built more than a hundred years ago by one of Glenfield's original settlers. Besides being a National Historic Landmark, it was used as a location for a movie. Sam even got a big part. All I got was to clean bird cages and double as a stunt dummy, but that's another story.

We climbed the steps of the giant white house. Sam knocked on the door. No answer. She tried again.

Boots approached on the hardwood floor. The brass doorknob turned. Colonel Pike peeked through the crack and grumbled. "Not again. Why don't you kids leave me alone?"

I dropped my head and moped down the stairs. The IQs followed me.

All except Sam. For some reason she said the rhyme anyway. "Iggy, Iggy, Iggy, have you seen my piggy?"

When Colonel Pike answered, I nearly flipped. "Orky, Orky, Orky, yes I've seen your porky."

I spun around and jumped four steps at once. "Yes! Yes!"

Colonel Pike swung open the door and slapped his knee. "What in tarnation? You're round and red as a cherry."

Everyone laughed. But not for long. We didn't have time. Colonel Pike understood and quickly gave me my object. A tail. It was brown and long. He pinned it to the long johns.

"Don't pop yourself," he warned.

I told him not to worry. We had come too far to mess it up now.

"Maybe we already have," Chet said.

"Huh?" I asked.

He showed me his watch, 9:57 p.m. We had three minutes to get back to church or we would be disqualified. Our Felix stretcher was fast, but not that fast.

"It's over," I said. "We fought the good fight. We just didn't finish the race."

Colonel Pike stood up. "Now, hold on there. How 'bout I fire up ol' Dixie and take you back myself."

"Can't," Chet said. "The rules say we can't use any motorized transportation to search for clues."

"You ain't searching for clues. You're done," Colonel Pike argued. He didn't wait for a reply. He pushed past us for the back door. His cowboy boots clomped on the hardwood floor. We followed him to the barn out back.

"What's ol' Dixie?" Mitch asked. "A horse?"

"A horse?" Colonel Pike muttered. "What kind of fool notion ..." He took hold of the giant door and slid it open.

A thin layer of dust covered an old black pickup truck. Brackets held the headlights next to the hood. Spoke wheels filled the center of the thin tires.

"Hop in," Colonel Pike said.

We put Felix in the cab next to the colonel. The rest of us headed for the open bed.

"Are you sure this thing runs?" Crusher asked.

Colonel Pike just laughed.

I was still climbing in when he gunned it, with one foot on the bumper and a hand on the tailgate. "Stop!" I wailed.

He did. Too soon. I rolled into the front of the bed.

"Go!" Mitch said. "He's in."

I was in, but not attached. The inner tube around my waist didn't help either. I slid back to the tailgate. Good thing it was closed. When Colonel Pike turned, I rolled to the side. I bumped into Sam and she pushed me back. Colonel Pike must have beefed up his engine because we were flying. He turned and stopped, accelerated and skidded. All the while I bounced around like a sock in a dryer.

My friends were no help either.

"Coming your way," Megan said. She shoved me toward Crusher. He used his feet to roll me toward Mitch. Mitch sent me to Chet.

"Fore!" Chet called out. He drove me at Sam.

She sent me for a ride. "They don't call me Grand Slam Stewart for nothing."

"Uncle! Uncle!" I yelled. I decided to cling like Velcro to the next person I bumped into. That turned out to be Megan. Our eyes met. My face felt suddenly hot. Megan smiled. I smiled back. For some reason I didn't notice that the bumping had stopped. So had the truck.

"What a cute couple," Sam teased.

"Ah ... ain't that sweet?" Crusher added.

Colonel Pike and Felix hopped out of the cab.

"Pardon me for interrupting," Colonel Pike said. "But we're here."

I glanced around. Orville and the other SPs gathered around the truck. So did the other kids from the Lock-In, along with Joe, our youth pastor.

I realized my arms were still around Megan.

So did everyone else.

⑪

Is This Thing On?

I squeezed through the crowd for the sanctuary. Everyone pressed close to give me a hard time. The fact that we were the last team to arrive didn't help. My friends were in the parking lot waiting.

"Smooth, Willie," Joe said. He wanted to know if Megan painted the hearts all over my long underwear.

"They look cute on you," Stacey Brittle added.

"Make way for Prince Charming," Chet told them as he parted the crowd.

"Cutie Pie, coming through," Sam announced.

Colonel Pike hung back to talk with Joe, our youth pastor. I couldn't tell if we would be penalized or not. Not that it mattered. With only seven of eight clues, we didn't stand a chance.

"Almost there, Hunk," Chet said. He held open the door so I could squeeze through.

We moved through the foyer into the sanctuary. Teams sat together in the pews. I waddled after the IQs to the front, getting a few high fives on the way.

"Finally," Mitch said. "It took you long enough."

I glanced at Megan. As soon as our eyes met, she looked away.

Crusher didn't even notice I had come in. He just stared at the floor and wrung his hands. He wasn't about to make eye contact with anyone. When Sam asked him if he was okay, he barely nodded.

"At least we finished on time," I said, trying to see the bright side of things. I couldn't believe how quickly Crusher's mood had changed.

He ignored me at first. Then he glanced up at the cross. "I don't believe I'm sitting here."

That explained it. What those thugs said was getting to him. "Don't worry about it," I said. "Worship is cool. You'll see."

Sam encouraged him too, but Crusher was done talking. He just crossed his arms and kept his head down.

A bumpy static came over the sound system.

"Is this thing on?" Joe was tapping the microphone. Kevin Harker, the sound guy, flashed an okay sign.

That was all it took. Joe kicked into high gear. "How ya all doing out there?"

Everyone clapped and cheered. A few teams chanted their names. The IQs just stared ahead, not making much noise. The reality of our dismal finish was beginning to sink in. The sanctuary smelled of sweat and grass. We weren't the only ones who ran from place to place. Joe read the team names one at a time. Kids jumped and cheered on cue. Some lifted their Clue Catcher in the air.

When Joe read our name, Chet jumped up and chanted. "IQ! IQ! IQ!"

One by one we stood with him and cheered, barely. Mitch got into it the most. Megan and I were too embarrassed over what happened to get very loud. Crusher never came to his feet. He even sank lower, as if every eye in the building was on him. Sam clapped and made noise, but not much. I could tell the weight of sharing her testimony had hit again.

Joe finished with the teams, then called the Clue Catcher for the Brainiacs forward. He wobbled up, making the most of his goofy appearance. He had on the same stuff as me, but with no writing on the long johns. He bumped into a mike stand and the podium. The audience loved it. He tried to give Joe a hug, but the tube kept getting in the way.

Felix leaned over. "Maybe you and Megan should show him how."

I let that go.

Joe counted the objects the Brainiacs had received. Their Clue Catcher made a big deal of each one and the team cheered.

"Looks like seven. Not bad," Joe said. "We'll see if that's good enough for the win."

Only seven. Same number as us. As least we wouldn't finish alone in last place. I felt better.

Joe called our team's name.

Chet jumped up and pulled me to my feet. "Go get 'em, Willie. Yeah! Yeah!" He put a foot on the pew and sprung into a back flip. Everyone loved that. Chet was definitely the biggest spazz our youth group had ever seen. I just liked the fact that the attention was being drawn away from me.

Then I walked to the front.

Joe grinned from ear to ear. "What happened to you?" He had me turn around for everyone to see. "What about those hearts? Huh?" The audience ate it up. "Let's hear it for Mr. Cutie Pie Prince Charming ... Wilbur 'The Hunk' Plummet!"

Everyone clapped and hooted. Girls screamed like I was a rock star. When I took a bow, some rushed up and fell at my feet. It was actually kind of fun.

"So Willie, how'd your team do?" Joe asked.

I gave a quick explanation of Felix's injury. Then I started to talk about our clues.

Joe cut me off. "Hey, Willie, you haven't seen a helium tank around here, have you?" He described what a helium tank looked like in case I didn't know.

"Um ... I'm sure it will turn up," I said. "Anyway, we ended up with—"

"What about a UFO?" Joe interrupted. "Have you seen anything that would resemble a space ship or flying saucer?"

The audience ate it up. I started to sweat.

"Flying saucer?" I repeated, playing dumb. "There's no such thing as flying saucers."

Joe razzed me a little longer, then let me finish. I listed all seven items.

"Looks like a tie so far," Joe announced.

One by one, each team's Clue Catcher was called to the front.

"Seven again," Joe said in amazement.

I couldn't believe it.

Our team started to perk up. Maybe we hadn't done so bad after all.

When the last group came forward, we held our breaths.

He counted out the items. One. Two. Three. Four. Five. Six. Seven.

The kid looked in his long underwear as if a last clue was yet to come. But it wasn't.

"Awesome," I yelled. "We tied for first."

"Yeah, with every other team," Crusher complained.

I had to admit that was weird, but it still felt good. The competition was over. Now we could relax for the rest of the night. No more stress.

Sure.

Joe quieted everyone down. He explained that we had found only seven clues because the last one was here. Its precise location would be discovered later in the night somewhere on the church property. The excitement started to build. Teams talked about finding it first. A few started to look, but Joe made us sit down. He explained that the person at the final location wasn't even positioned yet. That would come later. In the meantime, all kinds of great stuff was planned, including music, food, a message, some singing, and a testimony. He looked at Sam when he said that. She did her best to smile.

A break came before the music and praise singing. That gave me time to thank Colonel Pike. I waddled outside and caught him as he climbed into his truck.

"Your plan worked," I told him. "Thanks a lot."

Colonel Pike winked. "Joe went easy on you. I think Felix's foot made the difference."

I patted the truck. "This baby sure can move."

We talked for a few more minutes. Colonel Pike brought up how our youth group had helped fix up his estate so it could be registered as a National Historic Landmark. In the process, Felix and I, along with my dog Sadie, discovered some gold coins that his family had lost years ago. He thanked me again and started ol' Dixie. That's when he noticed Sam in his rearview mirror. "She okay?"

Sam stood in the parking lot watching up and down the street. I explained that she would be sharing her testimony and wanted her dad to come. "He's been away on business. Plus, he doesn't come to church that much."

"Is that a fact?" Colonel Pike said. He pulled around and said something to Sam, then left.

I went over to her.

"Are you all right?" I asked.

She said she was just getting some air. While she talked her eyes shifted up and down the street.

I put my arm on her shoulder and told her that I couldn't wait to hear her. I promised that I would be praying for her and she would do great.

Sam managed to raise the ends of her mouth.

When the music started to play, I said we should go inside. Sam wouldn't move at first, then gradually started for the door. She admitted that singing was just the thing she needed. The songs would take her mind off of her testimony and put them on God.

Just as I reached for the door, it flung open from the inside.

Crusher rushed out.

"What's up, Dude?" I asked.

He didn't answer. Or look at me.

He just kept going.

⑫

Taking a Stand

"Crusher, where you going?" Sam asked.

Crusher shrugged and looked around. "It's getting boring. I'm takin' off."

"You can't," I told him.

Crusher glared at me. I shifted my eyes. Some of the old fears came back.

Just then a counselor came out and reminded us that we were expected to stay for the night.

"No one's locking me in," Crusher mumbled.

I appealed to his competitive spirit. "But the IQs need you. We can still win. We're tied for first."

"Every team's tied for first. No way am I staying in there all night," Crusher said.

I explained that we wouldn't just be in the sanctuary, that we would be moving from room to room depending on the activities.

He shook his head and stared down the street.

Sam crossed her arms and lowered her eyebrows. "You have to stay for my testimony."

That got to Crusher. He looked at Sam. "I guess I could stay a little longer. For your test thing."

"My test—" Sam stopped herself and held back a smile.

So did I. It never occurred to me that even though we had been talking about Sam's testimony all evening, Crusher had no idea what that meant.

Sam filled him in. "I basically cover what my faith means to me."

"Whatever," Crusher said, acting like he didn't care.

The adult counselor came over again. "Inside, already. Let's go."

Sam and I started in. Crusher didn't. Sam pulled at his arm. He grumbled, but followed.

We joined our team near the front. Everyone was standing. Crusher made a point to be positioned at the end of pew. The sound of instruments filled the sanctuary. Voices sang out. Listening brought back memories of when Felix, Sam, and I had a band of our own. At first we wanted to win Battle of the Bands. That never happened. But we ended having an awesome time playing for a group of children at camp.

Like always, singing really put things in perspective. The Lock-In wasn't about winning the competition. It wasn't about inventions. It wasn't about how goofy I looked. It was about God. Hopefully, the kids here would grow in their faith in Jesus, or maybe kids would hear about Him for the first time. Kids like Crusher.

The piano and guitar played on. The deep bass thumped against my chest. It was awesome. Between songs, the leader reminded us that it didn't matter how well we sang. Flat, sharp, it didn't matter. God listened to our hearts, not the notes. The leader encouraged us to make the next song a prayer. I closed my eyes and sang. I prayed that God would help Sam and that her testimony would go well.

Before the song was over, something prompted me to open my eyes. I glanced to my left, then right.

Crusher was gone.

I started to leave, then stopped. I closed my eyes again. I prayed that Crusher hadn't snuck out and gone home. That he went to the bathroom, got a drink, anything. I asked the Lord to keep him here. I asked that his heart would be open to hear what Sam and the pastor had to say.

The band led us in a few more choruses and kids really got into it. The projector shined the words on the screen for newcomers. No one talked or goofed off. They listened or sang.

When the music stopped, Joe had Sam join him up front. While he introduced her, I checked the back of the sanctuary. Sam's mom was sitting on a pew ... alone.

Then Colonial Pike walked in.

I held my breath.

Mr. Stewart wasn't with him.

But Crusher was. They sat in the last pew.

Sam cleared her throat. "I'm really nervous, so bear with me." She explained that she had been a Christian most of her life. Her parents brought her to church when she was 5. "My Sunday school teacher told me that God gives us faith so we can believe in Jesus. Even though it didn't start to make sense until vacation Bible school, I eventually realized that God had been working faith in my heart all along. But that doesn't mean my life has been perfect or easy. For one thing, my friends make things pretty dangerous."

"Plummet time!" someone yelled.

Everyone laughed.

"Now that you mention it," Sam smirked. "Willie and Felix almost got me skewered by a spear gun, run over by a coin thief, and drowned by a tidal wave."

Fingers from the pew behind me nudged my shoulders. Felix's too.

"Then there's my family," Sam continued. She talked about her older brother who had moved away. He never went to church. She shifted to her parents. "They're great, just super busy—especially my dad. He has to travel with his job. That stresses him out. He doesn't come to church as much as he used to. I asked him to come tonight, but ..." Sam started to cry. I turned around, thinking maybe her dad had come in.

He hadn't.

Sam forced herself to go on. She sniffed and spoke through tears. She explained how much she loved her dad. She wished he could be around more. "You know what's so cool about God being our heavenly Father? He is with us even when our real dads can't be."

The audience didn't let out a peep. Wet eyes seemed to spread from one face to the next. I knew a lot of kids had dads who weren't around much. They could relate. Sam finished with all the reasons why God was such a perfect Father. He loved us no matter what. He provided for us. He taught us. He sacrificed His only Son for our salvation. He made us a priority. She closed with a prayer and walked back to our pew. Applause followed her steps. It was obvious she had helped a lot of people, and they wanted to encourage her in return.

Crusher included.

The praise band went into another song.

I saw Crusher quickly wipe his eyes on his way to joining us in the pew. He gave Sam a pat on the shoulder and kept looking at her like there was something he wanted to tell her. She understood and waited.

Crusher cleared his throat and kept blinking. "I haven't seen my dad since I was 5."

Sam gave him a hug. At first Crusher left his arms down. Then he allowed himself to hug her back. When they let go and focused on the band, I could see the wet streaks down his cheeks.

I felt bad that Sam's dad didn't make it. But if he had, Sam may not have shared what she did, the words Crusher needed to hear.

When the youth pastor came to the front, Crusher didn't leave or even go to the back. He sat with us. I thought he might fidget with the pencils in the pew or mess with something in his pocket, but he didn't. He listened. That made me feel great. It seemed as though God was working in his heart. I said a little prayer of thanks and started to relax.

Then, without warning, the youth pastor asked me to join him up front.

Fortunately, Joe asked all of the Clue Catchers to come forward. Applause pushed us down the aisles, so it really wasn't that bad. The audience got a big kick out of seeing us all together. We looked like a bunch of teenage sumo wrestlers in red long johns. Joe made a comment about what a hip and stylin' group of kids we were. But right after he said it, he rolled his eyes at the audience.

That was a mistake. When you are outnumbered by seven sumo wrestlers, you don't get mouthy. Someone gave Joe a bump.

"I'm sorry, Mr. Youth Pastor, Sir," the kid teased. "I can't control my stylin' tube."

A tall guy with huge arms knocked Joe the other way. "My bad. Sorry."

After that, everyone got in the act. Our teammates in the audience laughed and cheered us on. We had Joe in a sumo sandwich. He bounced back and forth while holding the microphone.

"May D-Day! M-M-May Day!" he cried.

A few bumps later, he went down, still holding the mike. "Thank you. Thank you very much." He grabbed me by my ankle and I tumbled. I rolled down the steps and bumped into the first pew.

"Pile on!" a Clue Catcher yelled. Some kids landed on Joe, some on other kids. Clue Catchers flopped and rolled. Jumped and bumped. It was a free for all. I ran up the steps and got in the act. Somehow Joe went from the underdog to the upper dog. He was having more fun than the rest of us combined. Good thing he had to give a talk. He finally picked up the mike and calmed us all down.

"Time for an interview," Joe said. He held out the mike so all of us could speak into it. "How did it feel to go around town dressed like a clown."

"Dumb," a Clue Catcher said. "You should have seen the looks I got."

Joe interviewed a few more kids and the answers were the same.

"Everyone stared."

"A high schooler told me to get a life."

"One asked me if the circus was in town."

"I felt self-conscious. I just wanted to hide."

Joe looked at me. "Is that right?" He acted like he wasn't surprised. He directed us to have a seat then addressed the audience. "Some of you probably felt uncomfortable just being in the group with someone who looked so ridiculous. You kept thinking, 'I hope my friends don't see me.' Or 'I'm glad I'm not the Clue Catcher.'"

Lots of kids nodded, including Crusher.

"Some of you might feel that way about being here tonight," Joe went on.

More nods.

Joe explained that he had us dress up in ridiculous clothes to learn a lesson we would never forget. He told us that many people felt uncomfortable coming to church. For many of us, it was a part of our lives since we were young. But not for others. For some, church brought feelings of insecurity. Being watched. Out of place. Joe paused and let the silence have its effect. "But with church it shouldn't be that way. Everyone is welcome here."

Joe explained that Jesus invited all to come to Him. He talked about how it was the outcasts of society that came to Jesus, the sinners, diseased, poor.

"Jesus didn't care about race or age or education. It didn't matter how much money you had. In Matthew 11:28, Jesus says, 'Come to Me all you who are weary and burdened and I will give you rest.' That's what the Lord promises to everyone. Jesus comes to us here in church, and it's here in church where we praise Him in return. Everyone is welcome here."

Next, Joe asked what it was like to search for the clues.

"Frustrating," a kid shouted out.

"I gave up," another said.

"Confusing at first, but then okay."

Joe grinned. "Point number two. Some people think that the Christian faith is the same way. It doesn't make sense. But just like the clues, what seems confusing at first will later make sense. When the Holy Spirit opens your heart to the truth, you begin to see clearly what was confusing before. That's how it was for me." Joe talked about how at first he didn't want to go to church. Other things seemed more fun. But then the Lord showed him his emptiness. "Some of you are there now. So let me solve the mystery about God."

He made it clear in one sentence. "Jesus died on the cross for our sins so we will have eternal life. God's done all the work for us. He even gives us the strength to confess and believe."

Joe watched the audience. The silence was amazing. No one whispered or fidgeted with anything. "There is a purpose for everything that happens in our lives. Very often we can't see the pattern. It's like that stained glass window behind the altar. When it's dark outside, like tonight, we can't see the design in the glass. But when the light shines through, then it's easy to see what's pictured there. Think of Christ as the 'light' which helps us understand. He's like the missing piece that gives the puzzle meaning.

"Maybe you've been searching for answers to some real important questions about life, and that's why you've come here tonight. If you're puzzling over things like forgiveness and eternal life, then you've come to the right place. The good news is that the puzzle is solved. Christ has provided forgiveness and eternal life, and the Holy Spirit brings us to faith in Christ."

Joe had kids bow their heads and close their eyes. He prayed that the Holy Spirit would strengthen the faith of all the kids at the Lock-In, and plant faith in the hearts of those who still did not believe.

When Joe finished, he asked anyone who was willing to hear and learn more about Jesus to stand. A ripple of applause followed a girl to her feet. As another new believer stood, the applause grew. I looked over at Crusher. He still wasn't standing with the rest of us.

"Anyone else?" Joe asked.

A boy near the front stood.

More applause.

"Great," Joe said. "Anyone else?"

Then one more rose to his feet.

Leonard "Crusher" Grubb.

A Middle School Miracle

A silent shock swept over the crowd.

But not for long. Hands came together. Cheers filled the air. The bully of Glenfield Middle School had just confessed that He needed Jesus and wanted to know more about Him. That the Holy Spirit was at work in his heart seemed certain. It was as if a miracle had happened right before our eyes.

Sam gave Crusher a hug. I patted him on the back. Felix rose on one foot and put an arm on Crusher's shoulder.

Joe had everyone sing one more song of praise. After that he dismissed the group.

Chet went right over to Crusher. "You did it! Awesome."

Crusher nodded. He looked relieved, but still nervous. I didn't blame him. He took a stand for the Lord in front of a crowd of junior high students. That would be hard for anyone, especially Crusher.

As we headed to the fellowship hall for a snack, Crusher asked me to save him something to eat. He wanted to talk to the youth pastor for a minute.

"Like a donut?" I joked.

"That never happened," he reminded me. He punched his hand as a warning, but couldn't hold back a grin. Then he stuffed his hands in his pockets and joined the others in front with Joe.

We stood around in the fellowship hall, celebrating. What an incredible night! We were still in the running for first place. Sam did great on her testimony. And Crusher believed in Jesus. Awesome!

Kids kept coming up to Sam and telling her how well she did. She thanked them and smiled, but her eyes betrayed how she felt.

"I'm sorry your dad didn't make it," I told her.

Sam pulled her blonde hair behind her ear. "Me too." She gave me a quick hug.

"Maybe God knew you'd share what kids needed to hear if your dad wasn't here."

Sam admitted that was true. Crusher was proof.

I walked around and talked to kids about how funny it was to cruise town looking like a blimp. They laughed and had me bump them with my inner tube hip. I gave high fives. The other Clue Catchers came together and we posed for a picture and the video camera. After that one of the adult sponsors came over and said we could take off our clues. What a relief. I felt cooler right away.

When Chet gathered the IQs together, he was as hyper as ever. "Can you believe we're still in first? We're going to win. Am I right?"

"You bet, Chet!" I shouted.

He loved that. He did a back flip in the middle of the room. "Willie Plummet is out of control!"

Kids looked at me, but mostly at Chet. I could tell I wasn't the only one who thought he was nuts. When Crusher came through the door, everyone applauded again. Joe had us sit on the floor, grouped according to teams. He told us we needed to encourage everyone who had just heard about Jesus and help them grow in their faith.

Next came a highlight video of youth group events from the past year. As soon as Joe killed the lights, Felix gave his backpack to Chet, then got up and left the room.

Chet noticed me watching and leaned over. "He wanted a counselor to have another look at his ankle. He'll be right back."

As the video filled the giant screen, I kept an eye on the doors, waiting for Felix. Minutes passed, five then ten. I finally got up and went to make sure Felix was okay. None of the counselors had seen him. I walked between the buildings and checked the youth room. No Felix. I tried to figure out why he would give his backpack to Chet and not keep it with him. Only one explanation made sense. He was done for the night but didn't want the IQs to be without our inventions.

I headed for the edge of the church property but didn't get far. An adult stopped me and politely reminded me that I had to stay for the whole event. He assured me that Felix couldn't have left without a parent picking him up, and that hadn't happened.

I stopped back by the fellowship hall. The video showed our youth group fixing up Colonel Pike's estate. Felix and I clawed at the dirt like animals, trying to get my dog Sadie to join in the act and help us. She didn't. Everyone laughed at the sight of us. I cracked up and turned my head, thinking Felix would be there.

He wasn't.

I walked in and out of buildings, calling his name. The night air cooled my face and felt good. But the darkness also made it easier for Felix to hide. Some of the adult staff joined me. We checked halls, rooms, closets, everywhere.

"Maybe we should call his folks," a counselor suggested.

I convinced him not to and to give me a little longer. He said Joe would have to decide.

I hurried away, mumbling to myself. "Where would he—" I held my words. Of course. One hard-to-find spot had Felix written all over it.

I climbed a flight of stairs to an adult Sunday school classroom. The darkness gave me the chills, but I didn't turn on the light. I bumped into chairs making my way to the far end of the room. I pushed at the window. Open. I squeezed outside and walked along the ledge. At the end of the building, I climbed the ladder to the top of the flat roof. Sure enough, Felix was resting on his back with his hands behind his head. He stared at the stars and acted like he didn't notice me. But I knew he did.

"Don't tell me," I said. "You're doing this so you won't burden our team."

Felix waited a while before answering. "My ankle's hurt. I shouldn't have to play."

"You don't *have* to play. We *want* you to."

Felix said that he didn't want to be the reason our team lost. He didn't want us to rescue him in the first place and now that we were tied, he didn't want to mess it up.

"Not again," I groaned.

"Winning is everything for you," Felix said. "You wanted to win the Bug Off. The surf contest at Tidal Wave. Battle of the Bands."

"There was no Battle of the Bands," I reminded him.

"Yeah, and who messed that up?" Felix replied.

I didn't answer.

"Me. That's who," Felix went on. "I'm always the one who messes things up. Remember when you ran for class president. I tore the banner so it read 'Willie for Class Sap.' Remember that?"

I help up my hands. "Believe me, I remember."

"Exactly. I'm done."

"You can't say that," I protested. "You think I care about winning that much? Forget it. Think of everything we've been through together. We built a float for the parade, captured the poacher at Lunker Lake, and stopped the Classic Coins burglar. What about when we shared my bedroom while your parents were out of town. Between you and all your stuff, there wasn't room for me."

"It was important stuff," Felix said.

I wasn't finished. "We both wrote for the school paper. We worked at the swap meet. We even died our hair green at winter camp together."

"Your head looked like a tossed salad," Felix pointed out.

"Remember when we both fell in Big Niagara at the water park? It was still under construction. I thought for sure we were goners. You know what went through my mind? I thought if I had to go, at least it was with my best friend."

"In other words, you were glad to take me down with you."

"No! Friends to the end! That's what I thought." I jostled his shoulder. "Friends to the end."

Felix shrugged.

"The thing is," I shared quietly, "This *is* the end." I joined Felix in watching the stars. "We have to finish as a team. Even if we come in last."

"We will," Felix said.

"Then that's what we'll do." I stood and offered my hand. "We'll be the first team to come in last at this year's Lock-In."

Felix stared at the sky a little while longer then grabbed my hand. He pulled himself up. "You bet, Chet."

Ten stressed-out eyes waited for us in the fellowship hall.

"Where have you been?" Megan asked.

Felix told her. I took the time to look around. Teams stood together in clumps, holding hands and whispering among themselves.

"What's going on?" I asked.

"Joe gave us the last clue," Sam explained. "It's somewhere in the church. We have four more minutes, then we go."

I looked at the clue. It made no sense.

Joe tapped the microphone. "Is this thing on?" He gave us a goofy look and laughed. I think he expected us to do the same. He thought he was a regular comedian. "Before you get going, I think you should see who's coming after you. Give it up for the Secret Police."

They marched into the room. But their freedom was gone. A rope wrapped around each of their waists and held them together. They moved like a giant centipede.

"Ooo, they're so scary," I teased. "Run for your lives."

Kids laughed and gave the Secret Police a hard time. The SPs loved it. They flexed their arms and backs like they were in a body builder competition. Some pointed at teams to intimidate them.

"You're going down," Orville said, looking in our direction.

Joe explained that the Secret Police would stay together for the whole round. They couldn't turn on lights either. If they tagged a team, that team had to return to the fellowship hall for three minutes. Then they could start again.

Felix raised his hand. "Are diversions allowed?"

"Diversions?" Joe asked.

"Yeah," Felix said. "Stuff that throws the SPs off our track or slows them down."

Joe had to think about that.

The SPs didn't. They flexed and pointed at Felix and talked trash.

"Nothing can stop us," Orville chanted. He hooted like an ape. For a moment I thought he would rip off his own shirt and eat it.

Joe calmed them down. He explained that any distractions that would harm the SPs or the church property were not allowed. "Get it? *Not* allowed. Otherwise, feel free."

Felix grinned from ear to ear.

"One more thing," Joe said. "See how the SPs are stuck together. Same for you. You have to hold hands when moving from room to room. If your hands come apart, three minutes in the fellowship hall."

Everyone held hands. Somehow I ended up with Megan's.

The IQs noticed and teased me like crazy.

My face turned as red as my hair.

Mitch shifted the attention to Felix. "Feeling all right?"

"Better than all right," Felix replied. He hadn't stopped grinning since Joe answered his question. He slipped his arm through the shoulder strap of his backpack and looked at me. "Let's show them what a couple of junior high inventors can do."

"Ready when you are," I said.

Felix hopped on my back just as the whistle blew
We were off.

"Let's do it!" I shouted.

Sam led the way, followed by Mitch and Crusher. I held Felix's legs and carried him piggyback. Megan held one of my hands. Chet held the other.

"Two minutes," Felix said. That's how long until the Secret Police started the pursuit. Groups scurried in every direction. It looked like a teen stampede.

Sam thought the clue led to the kitchen. We arrived there alone and scanned the counter tops. Nothing.

Crusher stretched so he could reach the fridge. He opened it with his teeth.

"Did you find it?" I asked.

"Find what?" Crusher replied. "I'm hungry."

"Time," Felix said.

The SPs hooted and hollered as they set out. Their voices echoed ahead of them.

"This way," Sam said.

"Give me a second." Felix opened his backpack and removed a sheet of glow-in-the-dark dots.

Mitch peeked out the door. "They're coming."

Felix placed glow-in-the-dark circles face down on the tile. "This won't hurt a bit."

"What good will *that* do?" Megan asked.

"You'll see," I told her.

We headed through the side door into the dining area just as the Secret Police entered the kitchen.

Felix chuckled as we hurried away. "Bingo."

Too bad the SPs heard him. They rumbled after us. We cut down a hall and slipped into one of the children's Sunday school classrooms.

"Do you think they heard us?" Chet whispered.

The door flew open.

"You bet, Chet," Orville replied.

I couldn't see Orville's face, but I'm sure he was smiling.

⌇⌇

By the time our penalty in the fellowship hall ended, two more teams had joined us.

"We didn't know it was the Secret Police until it was too late," a kid said.

A girl with braces agreed. "We thought they were from another team. I asked 'friend or foe?'"

Felix told them about the glow in the dark dots. "Just watch the bottom of their shoes. You'll know."

Both teams thanked us and said they'd spread the word. With that we were off again. Felix read the clue aloud. *"Put it on, then go."*

We talked it over and decided to try the choir room. It was next to the sanctuary. I led the way. With our hands together and the lights out, we moved like a blind caterpillar. We bumped into walls and planters. I knocked my shin good and nearly dropped Felix. We finally arrived in the sanctuary. A team passed us, laughing and falling into each other. Three more teams snaked between pews, searching.

"Secret Police on the way!" someone shouted.

We didn't take any chances. Felix climbed down from my back and our team dropped to the floor. We wedged our bodies under a pew. The other teams weren't so cautious. They jogged back and forth, making all kinds of noise. The SPs caught one right off. Then another. Teams scattered. Suddenly it got real quiet. We could see the outline of feet going up and down the aisles. That's when I saw the glow-in-the-dark dots. They stopped at the end of our pew.

I seized the opportunity and quietly reached inside Felix's backpack. I removed a bottle of my famous StuckTight 2000 glue and put a few drops by their shoes. The SPs shifted their feet and stepped in it. I counted the seconds. Five. Ten. That should do it.

"Try over there," an SP suggested.

Some started to move, but the ones standing on StuckTight 2000 didn't budge. Since all the SPs were joined in the middle, they tumbled like dominos.

"Have a nice trip?" I joked.

We crawled from under the pew and took off. This time we rushed through a side door and eventually wound up in the choir room.

"Just say it," Mitch told me. "Maybe we're in the right place and the person's hidden."

"Iggy, Iggy, Iggy, have you seen my piggy?" I asked the darkness.

No response.

Before we could decide where to go next, we heard the SPs on the move again.

"Everywhere we go, they go," Megan complained.

"That's it!" Felix said. "We're the perfect decoy."

"I don't get it," Crusher said.

Felix didn't explain. He dug through his backpack and pulled out a small tape recorder. He told the guys to make noise and stomp like we were being chased. Then he told Sam and Megan to talk like college counselors and say the SPs were cute.

Felix hit the record button.

"So what if the SPs catch us?" Sam cooed. "They're cute."

"Did you see the one name Orville?" Megan asked. "What a hunk!"

"Perfect," Felix said. He pulled the remote control truck from his backpack and rested the digital recorder in the bed. "Watch this."

Once the SPs neared the choir room, Felix hit the play button. We hid behind the rack of choir robes. The SPs barged in one door and Felix sent the remote control truck out the other. Our voices on the digital recorder filled the hall.

When Sam's comment came on, Orville kicked it into high gear.

"Did you hear that?" he sputtered. "I knew one of those college girls liked me."

The Secret Police hurried into the hall and kept going. We quietly followed. Once the tape ended, Felix maneuvered the truck to the side and let it sit. The SPs went barreling ahead and didn't stop. We retrieved the truck then checked a few more rooms for the last prize. Nothing.

When everyone was tired of carrying Felix, we agreed to carry him as a team. Chet and Crusher took his legs, Mitch and I his arms.

"I think I've solved it," Sam said.

We hurried for another part of the church—the offices. Holding hands and carrying Felix at the same time wasn't easy. Chet and Crusher moved apart.

"Not the splits again!" Felix squealed.

Chet told Felix not to worry. "I do them all the time."

"I don't," Felix complained.

We ran around, trying to stay close together. Felix really got nervous when we approached the flagpole in the middle of the courtyard.

"Look out," he yelled.

"Go to the right," Chet said.

"No, left," Crusher replied.

They barreled ahead.

"Are you crazy?" Felix squirmed.

At the last second, Chet cut left. "You weren't worried, were you?"

"No sweat, Chet," Felix squeaked.

When the church offices didn't pay off, Megan directed us back to the sanctuary. She wanted us to try the balcony. As we hurried inside, we noticed a group on the far side of the courtyard. Their glow-in-the-dark shoes gave them away.

"I've got one last trick," Felix said.

He had us pause at the pews beneath the balcony. He put the truck and digital recorder on the floor and hit play.

"Hurry up!" Mitch warned.

We grabbed Felix and climbed the stairs to the balcony. The moonlight offered just enough light to see the SPs move to the front of the church. The voices on the tape began to play.

"They're back there," Orville said.

The SPs hurried for the pew beneath the balcony.

Felix steered the truck under the pews to the other side. The SPs tromped after it.

"How'd they get over there?" an SP asked.

"They're crawling. Go!" Orville said.

I had to bite down to keep from busting up. Felix led the SPs all around. They zigzagged through pews. Went to the front and back. Finally, they ended up underneath us again.

"Watch this," Felix whispered. He sprinkled dust from the small container above the SPs.

"Ah-Choo!" one sneezed.

Another SP sneezed. Then another.

Felix elbowed my ribs and winked.

While the SP sneeze-fest continued, we checked the balcony. Nothing. We left and headed to our next guess. Still nothing. We searched room after room. The SPs appeared from time to time, but between the sneezing and glowing dots, they were easy to avoid.

Sam said the clue over again. *"Put it on, then go."*

"Speaking of go," Felix said. "I've got to go to the bathroom."

Sam stopped. "That's it!"

"Huh?" I asked. "With all of us holding hands, no one is going to the bathroom."

Sam shook her head. "That's not what I meant. The nursery. Come on."

We moved as fast as we could. Down a hall. Around a corner. We burst through the door. Empty. Sam didn't give up. She moved to the cupboards that held the supplies.

We could see a faint light coming from inside.

We flung open the door. Bingo.

Phoebe sat cross-legged under a lamp. Bags of diapers surrounded her. Finally, the clue made sense. *Put it on* was talking about the diaper. *Then go* was pretty obvious.

"Don't tell me," I moaned. "I have to wear a diaper."

Phoebe giggled. "No, silly." She handed us each a paper plate and told us to enjoy our reward. "That means go have some pizza."

I jumped up. "Yes, we did it! We won!"

Everyone cheered. I even gave Phoebe a hug and told her I wasn't mad about my long underwear.

"Are we the best?" Chet called out.

"You bet, Chet!" we cheered.

"I can't hear you!" he boomed.

"YOU BET, CHET!" we shouted.

With everyone holding hands, and Felix on my back, we paraded to the fellowship hall. I was ready to boast, but we didn't see anyone on the way.

"Everyone must be hiding from the SPs," Sam suggested.

Not exactly.

We pushed through the doors of the dining hall and found out the truth.

Time Flies

"Finally!" Stacey Brittle said. "Now we can eat."

Every other team had finished before us. We didn't come in first or even close.

The truth hit hard. Our hands came apart. We looked at each other as if someone should have an answer. No one did. Chet moved his lips, like he wanted to say something positive, but he didn't.

"We really did come in last," I muttered.

"I knew we would," Felix said.

We moped around. I moved from person to person, hoping to find an IQ with a few encouraging words. I didn't. So much for our great inventions.

Joe gave thanks to God for the food then kids lined up for pizza. Stacey Brittle grabbed two thick pieces of pepperoni and headed our way.

I braced myself for the wisecracks about how we finished last.

Stacey stopped in front of Felix. "Here you go."

"Huh?" Felix muttered.

"It's for you," Stacey said. "Without your help our team never would have come in third. The SPs kept surprising us. Way to go with the glow-in-the-dark dots."

Felix just stared at the pizza like it was a trick.

But it wasn't. Another kid came up. He spoke to me. "Dude, I can't believe you glued the SPs shoes to the floor. That was awesome."

When I asked him what place he came in, he said fifth. He didn't even know who came in first. And he didn't care. He just kept saying how cool our tricks were. And he wasn't the only one. Kids went on and on about our inventions. The fact that we never gave up on Felix really impressed them.

Crusher shrugged. "No big deal, he's an IQ."

As the compliments kept coming, I gave Felix a high five. We sat there eating pizza and laughing, wondering how a team that came in last could feel so good.

5:00 a.m. Darkness hid us from the streets below. We still had half an hour until sunrise.

"Nice spot," Mitch said.

Felix and I had brought the rest of our team to the roof. Since the pizza feed, we had watched a movie, sang with the praise band, made ice-cream sundaes, and played games. Right now, the kids that hadn't dozed off were singing karaoke.

"I still can't believe we came in last," Chet said.

Crusher shook his head. "I can't believe it didn't bother me."

"Sam's testimony made the night," Megan said. She put her arm around Sam's neck and gave her a squeeze.

"Leonard's silent testimony made the year," Sam added.

Everyone agreed and told him so.

"Just think, Felix," I teased. "Now you don't have to pay someone to protect you from Crusher, like when—"

"I don't want to talk about it," Felix interrupted. A while ago Felix accidentally hit Crusher with a water balloon. He was certain Crusher would get even, so he hired a bodyguard to protect him.

Crusher looked at Felix and laughed. "You're nuts, Patterson."

"You think that's funny," I said. "Remember when Felix wanted to name a comet after himself? He drank coffee by the gallon to stay awake at night."

"You never know," Felix said. He leaned back and gazed at the stars, using his hands for a pillow.

Our team joined him. We stretched out on the flat roof and watched the black sky, all hoping to find a comet for Felix. We gave it our best, but came up empty. Megan suggested that we look for shooting stars instead. I searched the countless points of light. Eventually, Sam spotted one. So did Felix.

"That's a start," I told him.

Felix chuckled. "I'll take it."

"It's amazing to think that the God who hung the stars, made us," Sam said.

"That's for sure," Megan added. "Every hair, every muscle, everything."

Crusher stared at his hands, trying to grasp the concept.

I searched across the building tops to Glenfield Middle School and said good-bye to Mr. Keefer. Then I listed the rest of my teachers one by one.

"I can't believe it's almost over," Felix said. He sat up and looked at me. "We'll never be junior highers again. Ever."

"Yeah," I added. "It's almost hard to imagine not being there. Like our lives began and ended at Glenfield Middle School."

"Cafeteria food," Mitch said. "What about the food?"

"Flag team," Sam said.

"The school paper with those cheesy advice columns," Megan moaned. "Who wrote those things?" She knew I did and couldn't resist teasing me.

Since I didn't have a good comeback, I decided to tickle her instead.

The IQs reminisced for a while. It was amazing to consider how much God had brought us through. As everyone stared in the silence, I prayed. I thanked God for always watching over us, for changing Crusher, for blessing me with the best friends ever. We had more than our share of misadventures, but He brought us through every one. Then I thanked God for solving the clue for us and giving each one of us the best prize we could ever get—Jesus.

When I opened my eyes, I heard a low rumble.

"What's that?" I asked.

Before anyone could answer, I found out. It rose above the fellowship hall like something from outer space. Balloons. Propellers. The Skyrunner 1000 had returned. And it was coming right at us.

"Quick!" Chet ordered. "Inside."

"You bet, Chet," everyone answered.

The Skyrunner 1000 zeroed in.

We stepped single file along the narrow ledge. The girls hurried through the window. The guys followed. Soon Felix and I were the only ones left.

"You first," I said. I helped him climb through then chanced a look back.

Orville stood in the parking lot next to his truck. He held the remote in his hands and guided the Skyrunner 1000 in my direction. It was too dark to make out his expression, but something told me he was wearing the biggest grin of his life. ✈

Collect all **20** books in the series

Look for all these **exciting WiLLiE PLuMMeT** misadventures at your local Christian **bookstore!**